I0762445

WHEN THEY CAME HOME

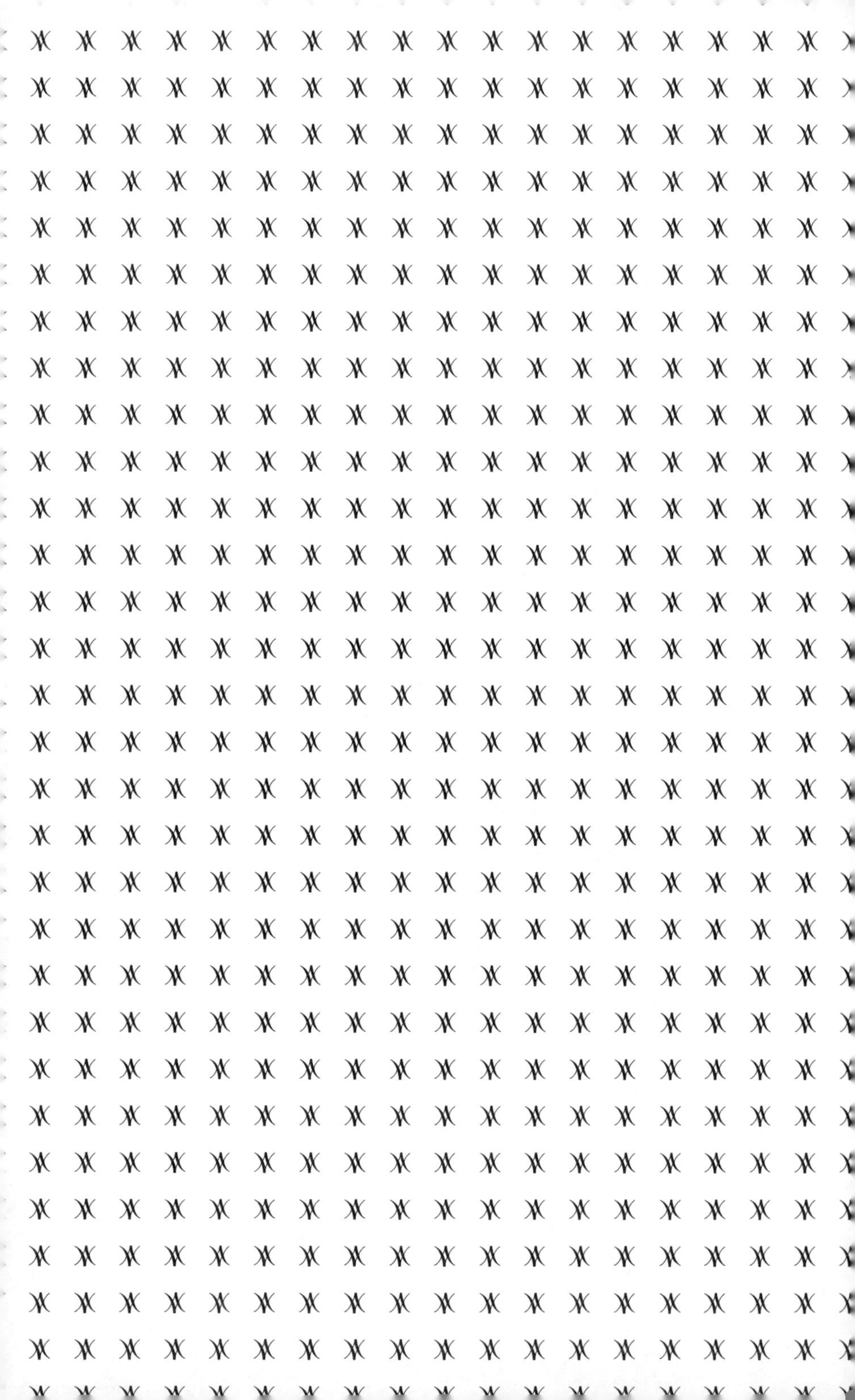

TERRI LEWIS

WHEN THEY CAME HOME

MIAMI UNIVERSITY PRESS

Library of Congress Cataloging-in-Publication Data

Names: Lewis, Terri L. author

Title: When they came home / Terri Lewis.

Description: [Oxford, OH] : Miami University Press, 2026

Identifiers: LCCN 2026000471 | ISBN 9781881163763

Subjects: LCSH: Post-traumatic stress disorder–Fiction

Marriage–Fiction | LCGFT: Novels

Classification: LCC PS3612.E9869 W44 2026 (print)

DDC 813/.6–dc23/eng/20260114

LC record available at https://lccn.loc.gov/2026000471

Designed by Crisis

Printed in Michigan on acid-free, recycled paper

Miami University Press

500 Harris Dr.

Oxford, OH 45056

In memory of my grandparents

CONTENTS

I lived in the first century of world wars.
Most mornings I would be more or less insane . . .

MURIEL RUKEYSER

War does not determine who is right—only who is left.

BERTRAND RUSSELL

WHEN THEY CAME HOME

AUGUST 1918, MILTON

THE ARGONNE, FRANCE

Milton's war begins with one long journey: train from Kansas to New York, ship to France, truck through the countryside, and finally just feet. He's twenty-one and has left behind his father's farm, days of plowing and milking, mucking out the barn. He misses Ol' Dan's greeting whinny. Also beds, dry socks, cherry pie. And Becca. In his pocket, the tiny blue feather she gave him.

First, the train. On board, how Company K laughs. How they eat! Townspeople at the stations offer the country's bounty: Indiana garden tomatoes, Pennsylvania home-canned pickles. Sugar's rationed so Milton reaches for sweetness. A square of fudge, a jar of jam. He shares his prize with his cheeky friend Herbert who waves and winks at the girls and who, if they giggle and turn away, pretends to cry. "We might not be back," he says.

The young men don't believe that. Stored in the baggage car are their guns. They have months of training and, packed in their kits, new union suits, jackets, boots. They are fresh in more ways than one, unlike the English blokes they are going to help, broken by years of battle, the Marne, Ypres, Verdun, Passchendaele. Company K crosses America, sprawled asleep in seats and aisles, waking at every stop, leaning out the windows, hollering, laughing, pounding their chests.

"They need us Yanks," Milton yells, thrilled by his daring, a daring he lacked with Becca.

"One week and boom. All over but the shouting." That's Oberly.

For three days on the train, when he's not sitting with Herbert, Milton walks the aisles, weaving from side to side, using what his mother calls his gift for gab and his father calls jabbering, spending time with other fellas. Behind him, the endless drilling in camp, but also the endless farm chores of chopping, sowing, pumping, raking. The train's like a holiday. Milton jiggles with the motion as he listens to stories. He meets a boy who loves pecans. A man, the oldest of thirteen, whose brother's somewhere on the train but they ain't talking. A kid who lied about his age to get in on the glory. Sometimes he stands by Peter, called Socks because he seldom wears his boots. Boys pass, hold their noses, swat his feet off the seatback.

"Got no manners, those fellas. Their mamas shoulda taught them better." Milton rubs his hair. "I hate boots too. They hurt my ankles."

"I was always barefoot." Socks shrugs.

"Toes wiggling in warm dirt." Milton lurches as they round a curve.

"Squishy pond mud." They grin at each other.

Outside spring unfurls, mint green and passionate. Fields of early wheat row past, a stray windmill, a cluster of grain elevators. Missouri, Illinois, Indiana, Ohio. Milton brushes the feather and scans the passing land for horses. Thinks of Ol' Dan. The soft muzzle, the nicker and nudge for a carrot. Becca, also soft. Her cheek, the quiver of her eyelashes.

One morning he wakes to the smell of pickles and farts; also a thought like a charley horse. He puts his head out the window where wind lifts his hair and roars in his ears. The thought remains.

When he pulls his head in, Herbert's awake. Crossing his arms, Milton leans back casual-like on the rigid train seat. Says, "You ever see a dead body?"

"Our milk cow got the bloats and keeled over," Herbert yawns.

"Not an animal. I seen those." His bowels clench. "A person."

"Like as not. All four my grandparents died." Herbert fist-scrubs his eyes awake.

"Was they laid out in coffins?" The most direct words he can find. They don't ease him as he hoped.

"Stiff as boards. Ma made us kiss them goodbye." Herbert swats away the memory.

"I reckon some of us are gonna die. We'll see bodies." There; said.

"How could we miss?" Herbert squints at Milton. "You ain't scared?"

"Naw." Milton realizes he cannot say fear-death-pain, not

even to his best friend. "The Huns are gonna get what they deserve."

"Hell yeah." Herbert relaxes. "I ain't got a problem with dead bodies as long as they ain't mine. Strung over barbed wire like we seen in the papers. That's not for me."

"You'd be dead." The kid behind laughs, har, har, har. "Dead, you ain't gonna see nothing."

"Lookin' down from heaven I might," says Herbert.

"More'n likely lookin' up from hell, soldier!"

Laughter rackets over the rocking of the train.

They have one day in New York before they ship out, walking up and down crowded streets, light everywhere, more people than twenty Missouri towns. Milton eats steak, mounds of potatoes, cherry pie—not as good as his mother's. He gapes at girls, the short hair, short skirts, legs and ankles everywhere; wishes he'd kissed someone (Becca) before he left. Late at night, he and Herbert drink just for the feel-good of it—his first whiskey, first port—never turning down the booze that flows toward them from older fellas who have to stay home, missing out on a free trip to Europe, a place of art and pansies, but now blown into a more manly shape by fighting. Like a grand barroom brawl in a movie, but with sound. The drinks ease his twisty thoughts, his longing. The girls blur.

Next day, Company K straggles up the gangplank of the ship. New York drops away and soon they are starving. Not from lack of food, but from the smell of barf and engine oil, lying seasick in hot rolling berths at the bottom of the thrumming ship. Seven long nights of endless din and sway.

On deck for fresh air, Milton meets a fella with a strange badge on his tunic. "You a cook?"

"I take care of birds."

"Chickens, like for grub?"

"Messenger pigeons."

Milton's a skeptic until his new friend takes him deep into the ship where stacks of wicker cages are crammed, filled with feathers, eyes, anxious murmurs, and the fluttering heart of a bird. Thinking of the coop at home, Milton is comforted; he helps with the daily feeding, leaving his hands in the cages longer than necessary, letting life scratch and peck at him.

On the eighth day, Company K jostles off the ship, tramps for an hour, then bivouacs for the night. Stunned by silence, Milton sleeps deeply and wakens to France, which is so foreign he feels he's tilting. Not only land after days of water, but soft green hills, delicate flowering trees, light that reminds him of attics. He marches toward the front lines, past rolling fields filled with unknown crops, so unlike the acres of wheat on the plate that is Kansas. Bridges of stone arch over rivers. Tiny castles nestle here and there. Villages. He's inside the fairy tales his mother read to him when he was small.

Milton squeezes his hands into fists when he notices how the clomp of boots and the thud of horse-drawn wagons seem to damage the countryside. Such thoughts are for weaklings and pantywaists. He's determined to be brave, to defend these little villages, especially the women who work outside the houses or in the fields. Their presence knots his gut, but they don't look up as Company K tramps past; they simply stop raking, sweeping, plowing. Only the children look; a brave one might wave. Milton regrets he has no candy to offer—he loves children, their innocence so like kittens—but he ate the chocolate from his tin of emergency rations the first day.

During one of the frequent halts, he says to Herbert, "They ain't got barns. Where they keeping the animals?"

"In their houses." Herbert shrugs out of his pack.

"The dickens." The smell of horse and pig muck.

"Oberly said."

"He's pulling your leg."

"Nope." Herbert grins. "He barged in a house after a little Frenchie he seen carrying a stick of bread. Pigs and goats lolling right inside the door. He reckoned the family lived upstairs."

Milton wishes he'd seen the girl with the bread. Wishes he had Oberly's nerve. The farm girls remind him of Becca, their long aprons and muddy shoes, hair pulled back, wisps around their faces. Their soft mouths. When he sees them, a feeling he can't name slides across his chest.

One morning he sees a wagon built for pigeons on a passing supply train. A bird hotel. Outlandish, but it perfectly fits the life he now lives, marching through a peaceful countryside toward a war. Afterwards, he notices all things winged: the spray of starlings settling into the black trees at night. Overwhelming morning song. A soldier carrying feathered messengers in a wicker pack.

They near the front and the weather worsens. Rain runs into their packs, ruining stashes of cigarettes. Boots squish; socks molder. Water drips off their earlobes. They stand aside for a line of tanks, new-fangled machines that struggle in the muck and mud that is the road, their guns like terrible arms. They remind Milton of threshers, the danger in them. When the hulks halt, the rain patters on. From the column's front, grinding wheels, loud curses, a call for horses.

A tank stops in front of Milton and a small round covering slides open. A hand emerges, gripping a bird. Released, the bird circles back the direction they have just marched. Flying home. Milton feels its escape. As do the men, who joke around their feelings.

"Wanna bet on that message?"

"Help, we're stuck."

"Send grub."

"Send sandbags."

"Send gals."

Milton had seen a girl just that morning, running through the rain, old newspaper over her head, bare feet splashing mud. He wanted to stop and tease—*What's your hurry, don't get mud on your pretty blue skirt*—but the column marched steadily on. "Think she was running to her lover?" For some reason, his chest ached.

"More'n likely the outhouse," Herbert said.

Just before they reach the front, a German plane overflies the company, circling so close that moving air brushes Milton's cheek. Men flee for cover, but Milton only stares: man turned into bird, muffler ends flapping like small wings, huge goggle eyes. The pilot leans out, shooting with a pistol and two men drop into the mud. Oberly. Milton rushes to him, but his friend is dead. As he leans over to brush mud from his friend's cheek, the grinning face of the pilot looms, and in a burst of fire, Milton's shot. He staggers, gasps. Nothing hurts at first, so he begins to run, but then pain sparkles up his leg, electric, red. He can scarcely breathe. His father warned him time and time again to be careful, the thresher, the danger. He falls. Sky, shouts, faces, motion. Socks drags him to cover. The pain spreads, a morass of red. He passes out and wakens to a nursing sister amazed at his luck. An iron fork deflected a shot to his chest. She hands it to him as a keepsake. Even mangled, he needs it to eat. Two days' respite, then bandaged, limping, gun in hand, he's sent back to the trenches on a supply wagon. His helmet has been misplaced. He finds one beside the road. Tries not to think of the head it once covered. The feather has been lost.

When flares of war appear beyond the horizon, the men stop joshing. Milton feels the deadly thunder in the ground or maybe it's his own trembling. He thinks of Oberly's body sprawled in the mud, then on a stretcher, then in a box on a ship home. No goodbye, no celebration. Just dead.

Late at night, Company K falls into the front-line trenches, piles of sandbags, wood supports, mud, the stink of men, puke, blood. From across a rubbled field, cannons roar, flinging shells over rolls of barbed wire. The men huddle against the endless hurtling death, bombs Milton comes to identify by sound. Whizz-bangs. Big Berthas. The names light-hearted, unlike the heaviness he feels as friends are carried away on stretchers.

Day after day the blasting fills his head until he feels the sound must spill out his mouth, his eyes, his gut. When mustard gas seeps yellow under the firestorm of noise, he wears his mask, breath rasping, vision encased. He imagines himself a badger hiding from dogs. He's waiting, they are all waiting for a battle that never comes. The line has held for months. Stalemate. In this endless time, they play cards. As Socks deals, he says, "Hear about Austin? Sent back to medical. Crazy, shaking so's he cain't even walk."

"Funking it, the little shit." Herbert lays down a bent queen.

Socks trumps. "Send the weakling home. He ain't no good to us."

Milton envies Austin, eating soup, writing on dry paper. Maybe stretched out in a hot bath. He grips his cards. Pats the pocket with his letters and imagines his mother under the swinging lamp, cutting pie. Yellow light; sweet cherries. Overhead, the French sky is bruised with cloud; the Missouri sky of his memory is always clear; the days silent but for birdsong and his mother's voice calling him to supper. He loses a hand, no good at bluffing. The girl in the blue skirt—*Becca!*—flirts through his thoughts; her warm cheek and soft lap. He could lay down his head. Later he sleeps restlessly in the nightmare world.

He wakens to fresh bombardment. A Big Bertha falls five hundred yards down the trench, killing Socks and three others. Bloody lumps, once men, are placed on stretchers. Bits of skin merge with the filth on his uniform. The waiting gnaws into his wounds. *I'm going to die. Get it over with.* He imagines a shiny coffin in church, his weeping mother, his father stern and sorry. He wants to put Becca in the picture, tears on her soft cheeks, but no, her last letter came weeks ago. He has hoped they were simply lost in the chaos, but now he thinks he will die wifeless, childless. Unkissed. Praying to be wrong, he covers his face with his arm and manages to sleep again, dreaming he is home, lying in a barn beside a sweet-faced sheep.

"Something's up," Herbert yells in his ear.

He's half-awake, leaning against a sandbag and fumbling with ammunition. Overhead deadly comets careen. Company K is alert, coiled under the edge of the trench, waiting for an order. Caught in a white rapids of fear, Milton wills himself away from the howling bombs that pulverize every living thought. Tries to imagine Becca's face. His fingers shake on the cold gun, and Herbert, crouched next to him, claps his friend on the back. "This is it, Miltie. The real war." Milton steadies. The command to fire must come at any time, and he thinks he can do this. He can kill.

"Huns! Here they come."

Just as the dark figures emerge from the far side of the field, running, firing, leaping like crazed stags over the barbed wire, Herbert cries out. Milton turns. Catches him by the shoulders. His face! Lips pulled back. Eyes dark and frantic. Blood pouring from his neck. Milton clutches the limp body as it skids down his tunic, smearing hot red. He screams for a medic but now: "Fire, fire!"

He's shaken by a spasm of shooting, no aim, just pouring fear out with the bullets, feet tangled in Herbert. Men fire like animals, frenzied, screaming, bleeding, toppling. The trench dissolves into arms and legs and crimson mud. Then, as the black figures begin to fall back from the rage of guns, comes the order: "Over the top."

Milton kicks away the body that was Herbert, slips, is pushed from behind. Onto the field, running, shooting. Shit in his pants, blood everywhere. He trips, falls into a shell hole. Ears ringing, eyes fisted shut, his longing for Becca, the green of winter wheat on the farm, Ol' Dan, obliterated. He is nothing, no one.

AUGUST 1919, EDITH

ENTERPRISE, KANSAS

When the organ starts the prelude to worship and the wooden pew vibrates with the low notes, Edith leans back. She hopes her soul will awaken like the wood because she is a sinner and God knows it. As does her mother, who says she thinks too much to be godly. Like today. Instead of praying, she's thinking of her brother who's coming home and bringing two friends to work in the fields. The new men are back from the Great War in France—thank God that's over and they are safe, her mother had said—and because jobs are scarce, they're going to help out on her father's farm. Will she like them? Will they be tall? Will they like her? Good heavens, she's in church, such unsuitable thoughts, even though marriage is sacred and takes place in a church. She prays to be married and tries not to think about the part of marriage that takes place in bed. She feels herself blushing. Vows to stop her unholy thoughts.

Up in the windows, light cascades through stained glass. Jesus's robe is a deep, rich red, and Edith wishes for a velvet dress of that hue. It would set off her pale skin and dark hair, but where could she wear such a dress?

She glances at her best friend, sitting across the aisle with her own family. Hortense might wear velvet if she marries Clarence because Clarence's father owns the Enterprise Mercantile and travels to Florida and Kansas City, where there are parties and . . . stop thinking. *Lord, make me mindful of your blessings.*

As the congregation rises to sing the first hymn, Edith's brother, Ed, troops in with his wife and baby, followed by the two new men. Edith lowers her eyes but glances sideways. Ed and his family edge into the far end of Edith's pew; the strangers stand a few rows down with some of the unmarried fellows whom her father calls gay blades because they stick a piece of wheat in their hatbands, whistle and smoke on the street, and wink at girls. They don't wink at her.

Because her nose is too big.

She sings, "*All people that on Earth do dwell.*" The other women in the church hold their hymnals and lean into their husbands or sweethearts. Her whole body is too big. Too tall, too wide, too heavy. She will never . . . stop thinking. Just sing. "*Come ye before Him and rejoice.*" God doesn't care.

The hymn ends and they sit for the Old Testament reading. The pastor has only read a few sentences when her mind slides from Judges, chapter five, to a pale pear cut in half and placed on her face. That's her nose. *Bulbous.* She has never said that word out loud, but in her mind she has never used it in any other context.

Edith glances again at Hortense, turned sideways and listening to the pastor, small and pious with a petite nose, upturned, perfect for flirting, which Hortense does effortlessly, even though Edith's father says the word is vulgar. With some satisfaction, Edith notes her friend wears white touched with fluttering lace like all the other young women in church. Hortense may have been the most popular girl when they graduated from Enterprise High, but she can't sew. Edith is proud—no, she won't think proud, she'll think blessed—to be wearing a new jacket, lavender with four big buttons marching down the lapels. Mindful of the visitors, she stayed up late to finish it even though her fingertips were shriveled and she had a burn on her wrist from putting up pickled watermelon all day.

The pastor finishes his reading from Judges—"*Then the land had peace forty years*"—and Edith says a prayer for continuing peace so that the new boys from Missouri may stay in town. "Here endeth the lesson for the day." Stop thinking.

The congregation stands for the reading from the New Testament and her brother's baby begins to cry. The pastor intones, "The Lord be with you," the congregation answers, "And with thy spirit," and Ed carries his crying baby up the aisle and outside. One of the new men turns to look. He is astonishingly handsome. Tall with wheat-colored hair combed back in a pompadour, not parted down the middle like most of the Enterprise boys. His brother, who doesn't turn, appears shorter, slighter, darker blond.

They sit and settle in for the sermon. The text for the day is

These things I command you, that ye love one another. Edith wants to be loved and to give love; some nights in bed she throws her feelings out like a beacon, but so far she has only her family. Her love is greater than they can absorb.

Hoping for advice, she listens intently until a drop of sweat trickles down her neck. In the stuffy church, the congregation begins to fry in the Kansas heat. Edith tucks her hair more securely off her neck with a hairpin. She could be loved for her abundant hair—twenty-five hairpins to hold it in place—no need for a horsehair rat to puff it up. She is certain every woman she can see uses a rat. Hortense, whose hair is somewhat thin, wears one of those new-fashioned turbans; she looks as if she has a gourd on her head, but the little curls on her cheek are adorable. She's a modern Kansas flapper, and Edith, she's an owl. It's her glasses. She should have chosen the wire-rims instead of the tortoise shell, even though the wire looked like a flimsy butterfly on her nose. Stop thinking.

After church, the young people gather outside in the hot sun. "Bless the pastor for curtailing his sermon." Hortense takes Edith's elbow and tugs lightly. "Such a lovely jacket. You and your prodigious talent."

"I even covered the buttons." She hopes she doesn't sound proud. She wonders where the new men are.

Hortense leans in to whisper. "Mother invited the new Warrenton boys to supper tonight. You must come and help me entertain. Father will bring out the magic lantern, dreadfully old-fashioned, and he talks so much about each picture, I could die.

Have the photos from our picnic arrived? Could you bring them?"

Last year, Edith's father bought a camera to take pictures of his prize bull and his new grandson. Edith finds the apparatus fascinating. Unlike the bulky machine in the Salina portrait studio with its long wooden legs, the Kodak is a small, leather-covered box that fits in two hands with a little door that opens to reveal a lens sliding forth on an accordion pleat. Her father has taught her to focus the shot by turning the button and has even allowed her to take pictures.

"They came yesterday. Do you think they are suitable for young men we hardly know?"

No matter how Hortense answers, Edith will bring only three of the five photos: a tree overhanging the angel statue in the graveyard, a basket of fried chicken, and her friends waving with the fields and town in the background. The fourth was ruined when laughter caused her to jiggle the camera and the fifth is of the mock wedding Hortense had planned, practicing for what Edith knows she hopes for with Clarence. One of their friends took the picture—Hortense insisted—of Edith playing the role of minister, wearing a choir robe Hortense had folded into her picnic basket with the deviled eggs. That photo will not be shown to a stranger; Edith wishes the new men to see her as a bride, not a staid devout spinster.

Before Edith walks to Hortense's for supper to meet the Warrenton boys, her mother reminds her they have been in the war. "I've heard our returning soldiers can be strange, so be kind."

Edith's breath catches; strangeness isn't what she wants, but she'll maintain hope. She pats her pocket which contains, as requested, the photos; she carries a jar of pickled watermelon. At her friend's house, the pickles are accepted with exclamations of thanks, and although she wishes to stay in the kitchen to help, Hortense's mother sends her into the best parlor, saying, "A woman keeps the men from swearing."

When Edith enters, she's offered a seat on the couch with its antimacassars. She sits stiffly, and once she has settled her skirt, Hortense's father introduces her to Milton and Wallace, the brothers come for the harvest. She performs the usual pleasantries—questions about the brothers' health and comfort on their travels from Missouri, the condition of the roads. No one mentions the war until, as talk becomes ragged, the recently signed treaty is discussed: the palace where it was signed—all those wasteful mirrors—and the dignity of President Wilson whose picture had been in the *Kansas City Star*, standing with three prime ministers and quite the tallest of them all. Edith listens and nods, fingering the photos in her pocket. These men will not be interested in a picnic.

When they are called into the dining room to eat, the long oak table carries more food than is normal for supper. The usual meatloaf, muffins, and corn pudding, but also cabbage salad dressed with cream and fresh dill, slices of ham, and little dishes of green olives, plum jam, applesauce, and her pickled watermelon. Edith supposes the bounty is because of the guests, and yes, as they settle into the hard chairs, Hortense announces she's made a peach pie for dessert.

Edith is seated next to Milton, a blessing since she needn't look into his face, for although she has heard women speak of harelips, she has not seen one and isn't prepared for his. It was repaired long ago but an uneven line of stitches wanders in a curve under his nose. If it wasn't for the scar he would be as handsome as his brother Wallace, who is flirting with Hortense. The same well-shaped nose and blue eyes, the same pompadour and small ears, although he is much the slighter. Edith passes the meatloaf to him and wonders how helpful he will be on the farm, then, abashed at her unkind thoughts and forgetting her mother's admonition, blurts, "I heard you were in the Great War. May I ask where?"

There's an agonizing pause, then Milton says, "In France. Much marching and waiting in the trenches for the fighting to begin. Nothing of great interest to a young lady. Especially now that it's over. Would you care for more corn pudding? It's extremely good."

Rebuffed and mindful of her mother's advice—*best not speak of that*—Edith accepts the heavy pottery dish and turns the subject to farming. To her relief, Milton responds, speaking with enthusiasm about cream test centrifuges and explaining how phosphorus improves the yield of the crops, topics Edith has heard discussed around her family dinner table and can appreciate. She asks about his family. In addition to Wallace, he has another brother and three sisters; his father works in a Warrenton bank and, Edith is astonished to hear, his uncle sells cars; except for the men who work at the Enterprise machine shop, most everyone she knows farms. Hortense's father sells dry goods on Main Street and her neighbor runs the soda fountain at the drugstore, but a person who sells cars? Exotic and truly strange, but Milton seems untouched; he's a farmer. Buoyed, Edith says, "Missouri must be overrun with automobiles." Cheeks burning, she forks a bit of meatloaf.

"No more than most," Milton says kindly. "There are still horses on the roads. I like them better than cars which kick up such an infernal trail of dust. Make frightening noises. Backfiring like . . . whizzing . . . startling to children and ladies."

She clenches, confused by his sudden shakiness, but then he smiles. She dares say, "I read in *The Enterprise Journal* that Dickinson County has one car for every eighty people." Change the subject. "Do you suppose that there will come a time when there are no horses?"

"I hope not. Horses are gallant beings. You should have seen them pulling the guns. Oh, beg pardon, I know young ladies are not interested in the war."

Edith wants to understand this man—he has been in the war, so what does that mean for his heart?—but feeling his hesitation, she asks if he has much familiarity with cattle. When he demurs, she speaks of her father's Herefords, their soft white faces and long eyelashes. "When I was quite young, I was often sent into the field to bring them home. Maisie was my favorite; she had the prettiest markings like country maps. Of course, cows are very dumb, but they are God's creatures and I love them."

Had she actually declared love for a cow? Thankfully, Milton replies, "I honor your thought. I have often felt the same about horses and dogs."

After dinner, the company remains at the table while Hortense's father goes into the parlor to take a large portrait from the wall so the magic lantern can cast its pictures freely. As they wait, Edith is asked to bring out the picnic pictures. To her surprise, as the tiny prints pass from hand to hand, the young men exclaim about the beauty of the statue, the fineness of the fields, and the fun to be had among friends in Enterprise. Milton is the last one to look at the pictures; he says little, gathering them into a small stack. When they rise to move into the parlor, Milton hands them to Edith. "They are well taken. I believe you have a good eye." His fingers touch hers.

Edith suddenly makes sense of an equation she'd been forced to memorize at school—the calculation of power at an electrical node: *Voltage = Current x Resistance*. Abstract before, at most an explanation for the lights that hang in her father's house, it flares into meaning.

Her hand is a node, as is his hand. They are young and vital—that is the current. There is resistance because they barely know each other and their families are not acquainted. Therefore, the voltage is considerable. She tries to breathe. Smiles.

As they stroll into the dining room, Edith feels how large she is next to him; they stand almost the same height, and she outweighs him considerably. She won't know until years later that Milton, who fights terror every day, feels safe and protected by her bulk.

Just before they sit, he says, "I have some pictures . . ." She smiles across at him. He takes a deep breath. "From the war, if you would be interested in seeing them."

"I would." The current flows on their words. His smile obliterates her, a memory she will hold onto in her coming life.

"I will call tomorrow evening then, if I may."

AUGUST 1919 TO JUNE 1920, EDITH WITH MILTON

ENTERPRISE, KANSAS

After their introduction at Hortense's house, Edith and Milton often walk out together. He comes in the early evening, washed and in a clean shirt, and they stroll into the late summer twilight, crossing the park, dipping in and out of the shadows, or following lanes surrounding town, where they occasionally pass other courting couples. Cows low in deep grass; the moon rises. She finds she can make him laugh. And although he left school after eighth grade—she's proud to have graduated high school—he talks easily of France where he served during the war, how the French farmers house their animals, the charm of the villages, and the grace of stone bridges arched over the streams. He doesn't speak of fighting, and she admires his reticence; also his industry: he never misses a day of work. At rough spots in the path, he offers his arm; she takes it and feels his heart's soft thump against his ribs. Such intimacy.

When harvest is done, he finds employment at the mercantile—she hopes she's the reason he stays—and they continue into winter, donning gloves and scarves against the wind. Nothing stops their talking. He goes home to Missouri for Christmas and when he returns gives her a silk lace-edged hanky with *Paris* embroidered in pink. She takes it as an omen—they will travel the world together—and folds it into an envelope by her bed. Their walks continue despite snow; they laugh and lean together, cheeks stiff with cold.

In March, the weather eases and they stroll further afield, past the greening winter wheat. One late afternoon, larks burst from the earth and he stops to say, "I much enjoy our time together." He hesitates, takes her hand. Breath gathers in her chest and she prays this is the longed-for moment. "I was wondering if we might." When he hesitates further, she nods yes and takes his other hand. He steps close and kisses her on the lips.

Electric like their first meeting when their hands touched—the charge, the circuit now complete. Inside the kiss, she wants to open her mouth and swallow him down, she feels he's so completely hers. He buys her a ring at the mercantile, and they set a date for the wedding: September when it's cooler. In the fuss that follows, she sometimes wishes they could simply marry at the courthouse, such weddings are now authorized by the state, but a church wedding will join her to Milton before God and she wants His approval.

Now, as the arrangements are made—women chattering about refreshments and dresses and guests—Milton retreats into silence. He is a careful man, avoiding noisy groups, always trying to fit in when among company, but his increasing reticence when they walk unnerves her. She might ask if he has regrets, but couldn't bear for him to say yes, so she pretends they are too busy with the wedding, there's no time to talk like before. Through the summer heat, as her mother and sister fuss over details, the cake and the trousseau—sheets to sew, pillowcases and dish towels to embroider—Milton falls mute, only speaking when spoken to or when politeness requires. They still walk as the sun drips into evening and leaves wilt on the trees; their footsteps ring loud where once were words. In the close, hot nights, she wants to urge his return but has no idea how. At last, the heat wanes into September, and her wedding nears.

The first of Milton's relatives to arrive in Enterprise is Malinda, Milton's younger sister, daringly traveling alone. Edith decides to ask her about Milton's childhood, his likes and dislikes, why he volunteered to serve. The two women sit alone on the front porch with glasses of lemonade and after some admiration of the perfect fall weather, Malinda says, "I'm so glad Milton found you. There was no one at home in Warrenton for him. Of course, he'd been sweet on Becca before the war." She sips, looking at Edith over the glass. "You don't mind if I mention her?"

Despite an inner quaver, Edith tilts into Malinda's directness. "Not at all."

"A real floozy to my mind. Always wore blue. To bring out her eyes, she said. I don't think much of a girl who admires herself, but Milton was minded to marry. But then off he went to France, doing his duty. When he came home with a silk hanky for her, she'd already run off with another."

Edith coughs to cover her gasp.

"All to the best," Malinda continues. "She was a flighty little thing. Not sturdy like you. Milton needs a wife with her feet on the ground."

Edith pushes down the hanky, hears only *sturdy*. She's not small, granted—and has a big nose—but the word implies a wounding lack of imagination. She has spent nights planning her life to come . . . their life: the house she'll keep, its braided rug and rocking chair, surely they can afford a rocking chair, a blue dish for creamed potatoes. And their children. After a long puzzle over possible names, she has settled on Doris and Walter William. She flutters a little at the thought. When the hanky rises, she pushes it away.

"I'm sure you've found out he's a talker. Going on a blue streak to anyone who'll listen. Jabbering, Dad calls it. He used to talk to Minnie, our cat." Malinda laughs.

Another jolt. She has forgotten the Milton who talked freely during their walks at the beginning, when she heard about Minnie, the farm horses, the rousing with Herbert in New York. After their engagement, he gradually fell silent, and now when she asks about his day or admires a slice of moon, he nods, offhand. Sometimes he turns to stare, as if surprised that she's there, his blank eyes extinguishing her. Then she stutters, snatches at another subject—the farm, the coming harvest, anything to bring him back. At night, in bed, she tells herself men are silent and he has simply grown into manhood, a state reached with the decision to marry her. Is he sorry, longing for Becca? No, no, she feels he's totally hers. Now on the porch, she throws off her disquiet and rises to bring more ice chips from the icebox. When she settles, Malinda says, "May I call you Edith since we are to be sisters?" Edith nods, although she falters imagining closeness with this confident woman.

"Thank you. I shall then be bold as to a sister: I admire you for marrying—the abundant cooking and cleaning and children. I myself am not of the mind to marry. I have just been taken on as secretary at the Old Soldiers' Home for Confederate Survivors outside of town. My uncle who sells cars has found a suitable vehicle for a young woman and taught me to drive, and last week I commenced to live in my own apartment."

Edith controls her eyebrows at this astonishing declaration. A single woman, living alone. Of course, Warrenton is full of her family, but what must the neighbors think?

Malinda goes on, "I'm saving money to buy a rocking chair from the Sears catalog. The plush seat and padded back will be so comfy after a day of work. My bones are not old like the fellers in the Home, but I will welcome the softness." Edith has to laugh, then they drain their lemonades.

That night she contemplates burning the hanky so as not to think of it again, but it is too pretty.

During the summer, Edith's mother despaired at the many notes of acceptance to the wedding; so embarrassing if too few neighbors offered rooms to her guests, but now all has been arranged to her satisfaction. A bewildering number of Milton's relatives disembark at the little Enterprise train station, a journey of over six hours from Warrenton. Edith goes with Milton to greet his parents and to walk them to her parents' house, where she has relinquished her bedroom for the sleeping porch. Her mother brings out their good china and serves slices of ham with corn fresh from the field. Edith herself has baked a cherry pie for dessert, hoping they will think her a proper wife for their son. His mother smiles, showing her teeth; his father pokes at the crust, chews on his mustache, then pronounces the pie excellent.

The crush of aunts and uncles and cousins demanding politeness and attention wears on Edith. She is fretting over Malinda's comments about Becca and wishes for privacy to question Milton. She'll release him from their engagement if she must, but on the day she takes her courage in hand, he presents her with a box of candy. Whitman's Salmagundi, in a fancy gold tin that features a woman with drifting blond hair on its lid. "Your hair is dark," he smooths his palm over the top of the box, "but I reckon you have the same beauty." He blushes. Edith catches her breath. He does love her.

Now it is her wedding day and Edith paces alone in a basement room at the church. Years ago, she attended Sunday school here, enthralled by the Bible stories told as the teacher moved silhouetted figures around on a felt board. In an early sin, she'd coveted the little brown donkey. Now in the stuffy room which still smells vaguely of children—whiffs of damp socks and mud—she moves under the high-set window for air. Rising on her toes, she can see the passing feet of attendees entering church. Patent-leather pumps, Cuban heels, polished men's brogues, saddle shoes on a child. Overhead footsteps announce a crowd. Her sister from Salina with her husband. Her mother's brother and wife all the way from Emporia, even though they had to change trains. Hortense will be here too; she has bragged to their friends that she introduced Milton to Edith, as if the marriage was of her making. Dear Hortense. Perhaps it's true, that first dinner, those tiny photos.

Because Hortense says it's unlucky for Edith to be seen in her gown before she enters the church, she steps back from the window. She mustn't ruin the luck of her marriage. Many things could go wrong, but she's determined to have a happy union like that of her parents. A wave of exultation. Her handsome husband, perhaps a house, not a rented room, and certainly children. She'll have everything that life can offer.

She says a quick prayer against the pride of her exultation and smooths her simple dress, fine muslin overlain with embroidered voile, sewn by her mother. She wears slightly tight shoes, a gift from her sister. Because she'll have to stand in these shoes throughout the ceremony and possibly at the reception afterwards, she sits, careful not to crush her skirt. The shoes are something new. Her mother's pearls are both old and borrowed. But wait, she wears nothing blue. She panics. She must be perfect so when Milton sees her he will think, *I made a good choice.*

Compose yourself. He won't care about the blue, just an old wives' tale.

She reviews Milton's family so as to greet them by name after the ceremony. His brother, Wallace, she knows; he came to work in the fields at the same time as Milton. Malinda, of course. Uncle Wallis sells cars, a rotund man with slicked-back hair; at breakfast her father said *oily,* and she'd shushed him. Wallis's wife . . . oh dear, Edith can't think of her name. There's an Aunt Wally, but she's married to someone else. Concentrate. She wants them to accept her. To realize it's not her fault Milton is no longer a chatterbox. She thinks he's contemplating their life together, then clenches inside the dress, acknowledging his new tendency to jump and run at loud noises. He says it's because of the war but that her presence calms him. Once they are together, he assures her, he will be calm all the time. She lofts another prayer for his serenity.

Her mother comes clomping down the stairs, carrying a small bouquet of three sunflowers and a few blue larkspurs. "Your father went out and gathered these specially."

Something blue. "Oh, thank you." Edith thinks she might cry. Why had she ever chosen to get married, to leave her parents? Her mother, once doubtful about Milton, has said she sees how loving he is, how kind. Edith clings to that thought.

"The house is readied for the little reception. The greenery's lovely and the cake? Oh my, Mrs. Dalton made one fitting to send you and Milton off to begin your happy life together in style."

The thought of that beginning—the bed—wakens a tremor in Edith, but no, she remembers his kiss, how her body had trilled. She loves him absolutely and will be a true wife, won't flinch away. She struggles not to blush, remembering the rush of feeling during their single kiss and, after, how she'd rubbed his palm with her thumb, trying to prolong her desire. At this moment, she feels a deep warmth toward him. Love. Honor. Trust. She prays she's not making a mistake, but vows whatever happens, she will make her marriage a success.

Her mother is fussing with her dress. "I think we best go up now. The last stragglers were coming in when I came down. I'll go up and alert Mamie."

Mamie plays the organ, not well but loudly, and Edith is glad the first moment she sees Milton will be covered by music. She prays to feel something wonderful.

As she trails up the stairs, feet pinching in the new shoes, hand sliding on the wooden rail, she recognizes her last moments as a daughter. Now all her attention and care must turn to her husband. She joins her father at the back of the aisle, her mother nods, and Mamie crashes out a chord. Milton turns, startled, face tight—eyes, brows, mouth—and he staggers back, shaking his head. Without thinking, she calls, "Milton." He stops, blinks, and when he sees her, his face opens with joy.

MAY 1924, EDITH & MILTON

ENTERPRISE, KANSAS

When summer tornado weather bears down on the town, Edith worries her husband will be spooked by the noise, by the dark clouds. He seemed better in the spring, but as summer has deepened, his nightmares have returned.

They are living in the little house where she was born. Four years ago, a reception in honor of her marriage was held here, the windows hung with greenery, slices of date cake and home-churned ice cream served for refreshment. Soon after the wedding, her parents moved to a newer house on Main Street, and kind and understanding about their penury because the government had yet to pay Milton's pension, they offered her the old house. Edith takes comfort in the familiar smell of the attic and in the front porch swing where she can rock her daughters; she finds loveliness in the arch between the two main rooms and security in the bookcases built into the wall. Mornings, she visits the post office—hoping for the government remittance but always disappointed—then walks the five blocks home. When she turns down the alley, the sight of her mother's black-eyed Susans growing along the back stoop eases the dread of her empty icebox.

The house has its quirks. The attic stairs creak in the night, waking Milton. The back porch slants slightly; Edith has to brace the old washing machine when she uses the wringer and because of the clatter, she can only do laundry when Milton is away.

Before breakfast this morning, grateful he hadn't wakened with hollering nightmares, Edith put on the apron sewn when they were still courting and electricity ran between them, but now at the table his gaze pierces beyond the house to marching and shooting and she knows the lavender checks will make no difference. As they eat, she holds the foot of their youngest daughter for the comfort of its wiggle and warmth. Milton stares into the black mirror of his coffee, slowly lifting his eggs, fork heavy from the weight of the war, a weight that worsens day by day, month by month. She has seen it in his dragging steps, in his increasing refusal to go into company, his night terrors. Her oldest daughter Doris sometimes runs away from him when he reaches for her, which breaks Edith's heart.

When Milton leaves for the fields, her worries deepen at the distant thunder, as if of guns, a rumbling that underlines the Kansas light glowing storm-purple through the kitchen window. She puts her youngest, Mildred, to sleep in the front bedroom; Doris, a wild two-and-a-half, plays lions and tigers, crouching behind the sofa and roaring. A puny sound against the flail of wind. *Please let Milton work through the day.* If he flees as he has done before, they'll lose a day's pay and she needs beans, rice, and bacon.

⋊

Wind whirls the wheat into frantic patterns, panicking Milton and the horses. It crashes into his chest and he tears open his collar, struggling to breathe, determined to keep working. Across the field, the thresher crew rides a steam machine belching black smoke as it cuts down the frightened stalks. He flees to the edge of the field, huddles, quivering. The stalks bleed and succumb, dying like Herbert. Like Oberly.

Over him looms a windmill, solid, offering escape. Rung by frightful rung he climbs; at the top, he clings to the wood, face pressed against the splinters. The sun magnifies the noise, the wind. The thresher approaches, an incoming whizz-bang. He clenches for the blow. It misses him, then passes. He steadies and lifts his head to look out to the world, the far fields, the dark break of trees scratching at the sky. Hidden in the trees, his house. His family. He needs them. They anchor him to the earth, but they are invisible. He imagines floating above the noise into quiet. Into peace.

⋊

There is no one Edith can talk to. Not her best friend Hortense, on her honeymoon trip to Europe, nor her mother, dubious from the beginning about the marriage. And certainly not her husband's Missouri relatives, who always mention how talkative Milton was on the farm. They have been ever kind, never saying a word to her, no oblique blaming, even though Milton has frozen into silence. Those less kind will blame Milton himself. She winces, thinking of old lady Wilmot with her prune mouth whispering over iced tea. Edith vows never to speak of her family's problems. *Please Lord, support me in my silence.*

She washes the dishes and releases the water; some days the sink drains with a chuckle, some with a witchy cackle. Today the old crone taunts Edith. She smooths her apron, fingers the lace into alignment. The witch laughs, evilness whirling up from the sink to join the sound of the battering wind. The screen door on a neighboring house bangs steadily. She can see Milton's shirts clothes-pinned on the line and splayed like shattered men and imagines him in the field, horror and distance in his eyes. Whenever that look comes, she touches his shoulder and talks to him about cows and wheat and his daughters' latest tricks, but today there was no time.

How to bring him back, to give him the sanity of his family? A family he swore he wanted, a family he said would bring him peace, never imagining the sudden cries, the noise and smells. Although he startles and flinches, he says daily if he didn't have her love and his children, he'd be lost. She believes him. *Lord, help me help him. Keep my daughters safe. Let their father be safe also.* She says, "Amen" and decides to bake cookies.

⚹

A windmill blade flicks a shadow against Milton's cheek and he startles, knees trembling, so high in the air. He wishes for Edith. Leans out from the top of the windmill toward town as the hands of the wind slap his back, his shoulder. His whole body vibrates, a shaking that makes it impossible to think. The grain sweeps into patterns, he strains to read the living runes. Hears Herbert's voice: "This is it, Miltie."

Below, field hands run, little ants fleeing the machine, their sweat-dark shirts streaking the pale wheat. They reach out their arms, shouting, afraid. The machine turns, resumes its assault, and he is out of the trench, exposed. The guns . . . he gestures to the sky. *Take me.* Black smoke dulls his vision. Danger nears. His pounding heart knocks him sideways, and inside a great cacophony, he doesn't look down, doesn't think. He simply falls into space.

⚹

Edith rifles through the wooden box of recipes for chocolate rocks, always Milton's favorite. She has enough sugar, barely. She has scooped the last of their butter from its dish and is beating it to pale smoothness when she glances up and sees the kid running down the alley, shirt snapping in the wind. He turns into her long backyard, panting past the tattered flowers. It's the Monroe boy, the skinny one with too-big hands who's working with the men out on the farm for the first time this summer. Pushing down her fear, she steps onto the screened back porch.

"Too hot for running, child." As she opens the door, she remembers he's thirteen; no longer a child, but too late, word said.

"Mrs. Fieth." He leans down, hands clutching knees. Something in his look makes her heart beat loudly; she bends to hear.

"Milton." Breath blows out of him, a dire weather. "I mean Mr. Fieth . . ." Desperate gasps. "Needs you bad." He stands and unsticks his hair from his forehead. "Dad said I should get you." He looks away. "Mr. Fieth is . . . you should come."

To the fields? What about the butter? As she stands, confused, small arms clasp her knees. Doris, no longer playing zoo, has skipped out onto the porch.

"Mama?"

With her daughter's touch, she realizes what has been said. "You," his name escapes her, "boy, stay with the children."

"Yes'm."

As she starts down the walk, her whipping apron standing in for screaming, she calls back, "If Mildred wakes, just . . ." All movement stops but for the coming storm. What? Do what?

"My sister's got a baby," the boy says.

Acknowledging his capability, her feet unlock, but before she runs, she lowers her head and shouts past the dropping sky and Doris's howl, "Pray!"

JUNE 1926, MILTON

JEFFERSON BARRACKS, MISSOURI

They tell Milton not to think about the war. Push away the mud and the bombs and the rats and the body parts raining down after an explosion. Herbert's face. Socks buried by a bomb, found dead with bloodied fingertips from trying to claw out.

Dr. E. specifically says, "If you want to get well, you've got to forget the war. You evidently were able to do that long enough to get married. Well, soldier, do it again. When memories pop up, push them down like kittens. You're a farm boy—you know how that's done." And he does; he has seen his father with the pail of water, so when Herbert appears, grimacing and frantic, down he goes. Down the yellow clouds of gas hanging in the bottom of the trenches. Down, down. He pushes and pushes, because as Dr. E. says, "If you don't get calmer, my boy, and stop that twitching and jerking and screaming in the night, we might have to give you the shock treatment," and if there is anything Milton fears in his life, it's electricity running through his body. He has seen patients with burns on their temples. Patients turned into quiet nobodies, unable to ask a question, unable to care about their wives and children. No! Milton struggles to keep his thoughts empty. It's not easy. The thoughts are constant, as if he were sixteen, dick in hand despite the preacher thundering that fornication is a sin without marriage. Back then he'd worried about blindness, but that worry is over now. He has fornicated with his wife who says it's love. Oh, maybe here's a thought he can keep, Edith, the soft welcome of her in his arms.

He wishes Edith were here in Missouri, but Dr. E. says, "She's not healthy for you. Wives may lead husbands to talk." And it's true, Milton has talked to Edith. After their wedding, when he woke her in the night with shouts, jerks, and moans, she would shake him gently, take his hand and say, "Tell me what you were dreaming." He told her about Herbert, his jokes, his longing for apple dumplings, but when he got to the end of the story, he could only say, "He died while we were together in the trench." Edith was a woman; women were sensitive; they shouldn't be told terrible things like the spurt of blood soaking Milton's uniform and Herbert's last screams that couldn't be heard over the sound of bombs. He lay in bed with Edith, squeezing her hand tighter than he realized, and told her jokes that he had shared with Herbert, told her about the oysters and the train and the ship named *Antigone*. Eventually the fog would come, and he could sleep again.

In the hospital, he hardly sleeps. Or eats. A perpetual headache makes it hard to see; when he walks to therapy, the yellow siding on the buildings shimmers in the heat and at the crosswalks he feels exposed, in danger. The nurses find him at corners, unable to move, hands flailing, legs shaking; they touch him gently, saying, "There is no enemy here," but most days he's forced to crouch, to catch his courage, then sprint to the safety of the next wall. The edge of a shriek escapes when he runs; he feels himself a teapot under pressure, about to explode.

When he arrives at the final crosswalk, he flails across the concrete and up the stone stairs to the massive brick building where the doctors work. Inside, he covers his ears against the sharp whine of the fans—"*Incoming, incoming!*"—and arrives at his appointment. The nurse silences the fan and he goes in for a brief talk with Dr. E.

"Still having nightmares?" The doctor signs a paper.

"Not so many," Milton lies. He forces his hands into his pockets and straightens his posture.

"Good man."

Afterwards he descends into the basement for his hydrotherapy, sinking into the deep tub, soothed by the echo of splashing water on the cement walls and the distant comments of the attendant as patients come and go, sounds unlike any in his past life. If his head is clear, he looks at his body, his toes little blimps, his dick floating like a submerged flower. It hardly seems alive, so drowned and white. In fact, he's surprised to see a body; his head and thoughts have become his whole self. Often the warm soak drifts him into a fog and he doesn't remember the walk back to his bed or the nurse who gives him pills or the relief of sunset in the hot ward; time is blank until he wakes screaming in the night, crashing from the cot to his feet and then to the floor, arms and legs scrabbling.

"For Christ's sake, shut up."

"Get that goddamned loony out of here."

"Ain't we got tents to put 'em in?"

Milton crawls back to his cot, searching for thoughts that are safe, thoughts that will ease his headache and let him sink back to sleep without ghosts or bombs or Herbert singing as bits of his body fall away until there's just a face and finally only teeth, clattering around a red tongue.

In the mornings, exhausted and trembling, he takes his shaving kit to one of the sinks and, as he shaves, searches for his real life. Some days he remembers farming, the hiss of the wheat and the twisty feel of walking in plowed dirt, real pleasure until a memory of lightning striking a fence and running along barbed wire to kill two cows makes him drop his shaving brush.

Today he reviews his wedding, a safe and wonderful day, the Kansas fall blazing up blue and cool, the wind blowing the smell of earth across the road as he walked with his brother to the church. In his mind, he stands under the stained-glass Jesus and says the heavy vows; he wants to regain the hope he felt as he was released down the aisle, anchored to Mrs. Milton Fieth.

Behind him in the bathroom a soldier swears and slams the door; Milton twitches the razor, then sees in the mirror he has nicked his cheek to blood. Terror surges; he stands frozen, towel in hand, the soap with its evil smell resting on the edge of the basin. His head throbs. A patient with an eye patch pushes him aside. "Let a fellow get on with it, Buster."

Milton returns to his narrow bed, threading his way through all the other narrow beds, careful not to touch a bed rail, a hand, a shoe. He sits, begins to dress. Pulling on socks, buttoning, his fright seeps away to wait like a wave in the sea. He feels sure it will return, but no, he finishes the buttons.

He walks to breakfast, ignoring the dangerous flicker of the yellow siding, organizing words to say to Dr. E. because he must go to town today. He has told Edith to come. He has to see her, to be in her safety and hold his little girls who might not recognize him. He's been gone so long. Months. In Dr E.'s office, he blurts, "I need to see my wife."

Dr. E. glances up. "Without even examining you, I can see you're agitated, all skin and bones. It's out of the question."

Milton plows on. "She could stay with my people. Not far from here. I could go there for visits."

Dr E. takes off his glasses and squints at him. "Do you think this is a hotel? Come and go? Like your stunt last week?"

The previous week Milton had gotten his first compensation check from the government. Courage in hand, he left the barracks, talking under his breath, railing at the government: Damn military (beg pardon—Edith hates a man who swears) left him in this mess, saying the problems stem from other than the damn (sorry again) war. Edith unable to pay the bills, writing of humiliation at the grocer's, taking the little girls to their grandma's to eat. His little babies. Milton had gone to town to cash the check and wire the money to Enterprise, missing his morning appointment with Dr. E, who even today reddens with rage.

"Why'd you pull a damn fool trick like that?"

"My wife needed money for my babies," Milton says.

Dr. E. seems to care little about a patient's family; he wipes his forehead and folds his hanky.

"That money was more important than the appointment," Milton explains. "Milk for my little ones. Socks. Shoes. Things to keep them warm."

"It's summer and damn hot to boot. Them kids'll be plenty warm." Dr. E. pulls his tie loose. "See here Fieth, you must concentrate on getting well. The government's not paying for you to gallivant off whenever you please. Pull that trick again and you'll be sent away."

Milton is desperate for permission to leave the base, but Dr. E. puts his glasses back on and says, "Out of the question. You stay put and follow my orders until you're well." He stands. "Don't waste my time moaning about your family. I've said before, wives and their endless talking are a hindrance to sound minds."

After his therapy, of which he remembers nothing, Milton calls Edith. "Don't go to Warrenton. Come straight to Jefferson City. I'll see that you and the little girls have a place to stay." She tells him what train she'll be on and then the living sound of her is gone. Now he must get permission to leave the barracks. Not from Dr. E. He goes down the hot sidewalk to the main office where a sergeant sits, leaning into the moving air of a fan and working on a ruffling pile of papers.

"Sir?" Milton tries not to flinch when the air zooms directly past him. "My wife is coming for a visit. I need to make arrangements over in Jefferson City."

"I don't recognize you. Are you allowed to leave?"

"Yes sir. But I need a pass." Milton wills his body still as the sergeant fills out the form and hands it over. "But this is only 'til ten! If the train is delayed, I may need to stay out all night."

"Under no circumstance." The sergeant peers through the moving air at the tag Milton wears. "I see you're a patient, Fieth. You belong in bed at night, not out wandering the streets." He puts his fist on top of the papers with a thud and resumes reading.

Milton folds the pass. He will be calm. When Edith is here, she will hold him and show him the babies. They will be a family, a normal family and the quaking will stop and they will go home together. The train's due at 8:15. He must start back by 9:30. Be in bed by ten. He can make it on time. Time. He will be calm.

In the ward he gets his hat. As he leaves, he feels light and cheerful; the yellow walls are happy as he passes between them, careful not to fling his arms or jerk, calling attention to his going. He has until ten o'clock, and Edith is coming. He doesn't want to spoil his luck.

JUNE 1926, EDITH

ENTERPRISE, KANSAS, TO JEFFERSON BARRACKS, MISSOURI

When Edith finishes talking to her husband and hangs up the phone, she leans for a minute on the oak shelf, face hidden in her arms. She can hear the thumps of her mother kneading dough and Doris rocking in her little chair. Outside, her father uses the squeaky pump. The house holds love, she thinks, exactly what she feels for Milton.

Is it good news or bad, bypassing Warrenton? Milton's family has seen how hard she tries to help him and has accepted her completely. She will miss the warm kitchens filled with talk and coffee, the girls will miss giggling with their cousins in the high beds, and she has never been to Jefferson City. No matter, she's packed, the girls are ready, and since it's Saturday, her father will drive them to the station in his new black Hudson. She's sorry the horses are gone but recognizes it is harder to harness a horse than to start an engine with a couple turns of the crank. "And gas is cheaper than oats," her father says.

She gathers up the girls and as she helps Doris into the car, she's aware of the row of porches on the facing houses across the street, friendly places where she has sat with neighbors drinking iced tea. Are they looking out, wondering if she'll be coming back? She imagines Milton calm, able to sit among friends like Hortense and Clarence without his leg at a constant jiggle, setting the glasses to clatter. Quiet talk without fear of a noise from the street—a car backfiring, a kid with a pop-gun—to set him running. He must be better. He has been able to get the government money to her and to call, speaking like any other man into the phone, repeating back the time the train is to arrive and promising to make arrangements.

Into the car they go. At the last minute, Edith's mother rushes out of the house and crowds into the back seat. "Bread's set to rise so I thought I'd come along. Give me the sweet little pumpkin." Edith takes the lunch basket from her mother and hands over Mildred. Her youngest is a blessing with sweet fat cheeks that make her eyes into crescents when she smiles, and she smiles a lot. Doris is another story; loud, feisty, independent. As if to confirm her mother's thoughts, as soon as they arrive at the little Enterprise train station, Doris stomps up and down the platform, pretending to be a bear, growling and swinging her arms. Edith is embarrassed. "Where does she get these ideas?"

Her mother laughs. "Let her get some of that energy out. It's a long ride to Warrenton. Keep an eye on her, Charles. I'll watch this little one."

Edith goes to buy her tickets, glad to be alone because of her changed plans. No need to worry her mother who has found Milton dubious from the start but who trusts his people. Edith also trusts them, but she must learn to trust Milton as well. Despite . . . she pushes the thought down.

As the train chuffs up, her father hands her one of his handkerchiefs tied around some coins. "Thank you, but I've money enough now that the government has paid us what was owing." She reaches to catch Doris's hand as she stamps past.

"None too soon if you ask me." He pushes the knotted hanky into her pocket. "Keep it. Wipe the little ones' noses and buy them a treat." She doesn't favor candy but her father keeps a little dish of jellybeans on his desk for his granddaughters, who have inherited Milton's sweet tooth.

She takes Mildred from her mother, balancing the child on her hip, and they board the train; her father hands the suitcase and the basket to a farm boy getting on. Edith trundles Doris ahead of her down the aisle; her daughter pats every passenger, proclaiming loudly, "Hi. We're going to see my daddy." Doris has her father's way of talking to strangers, which confounds Edith herself. She shoos her into the hard straw seat, but when Doris looks out the window, she sees they're on the wrong side to wave. She starts crying loudly, "Where's my grandma?" One of the passengers lifts Doris over to the window on the other side where she waves gaily, "Bye bye, byebyebye."

Embarrassed again, Edith settles Mildred beside her and checks the lunch basket, where she finds a surprise; her mother has tucked in a new book on top of her Bible, Edmund DuLac's *Fairy Book*. The stories are too old for the little girls but the pictures! The book falls open to a young woman trailing a red gown across a black-and-white tile floor in front of two golden elephants and a snake. Suddenly she feels a little less worried about this trip. Milton will find them a place; he's been to Europe and understands the world. The train begins to move from the station, and as Doris's cries reach a peak, Edith plucks her back with thanks to the laughing woman upon whose lap she's standing.

"How old is she?"

"Almost five."

"She's a darling."

Well, maybe. There's scant chance Doris will sit quietly for the entire seven-hour train trip. Edith grimaces, cleans her glasses, thinks about arriving in Jefferson City. She envisions a threadbare stained carpet on rickety stairs and bare brown rooms where men drink and yell. In a panic, she looks at the train schedule in her purse, calculating a return to Warrenton if Milton has failed, but there is no train until 4 a.m. She can't keep the girls in the station overnight. She wishes she had emphasized safety to Milton when they spoke.

Crowded by Doris in the seat, Mildred begins to whine. Edith breathes deeply, takes the child on her lap, and forces herself to smile. No need for them to feel her worries.

Three hours into the trip, they are shuttled off onto a siding where they wait for over an hour, nothing to see but grain floating in the heat. Mildred is sleeping, but Doris wants to walk up and down the aisle. Edith makes her promise to walk like a lady, but after two trips, when she begins skipping and laughing, Edith fishes her back and her laughter turns to wails. Out comes the book. Doris's sobs stop when the golden elephants appear. "Can you tell me a story about the elephants, the lady, and the snake?" Edith asks. Doris's story is long and involved and includes lots of "and then, and then," as if she's afraid her mother will turn away unless the words continue. By the time the Express streams by and they continue their journey, both girls are asleep.

Now they are going to be late. Edith stares out the window at the endless corn and wheat. Here and there a machine puffs through a field, throwing noise against the chug of the train. The later they are, the crankier the girls will be and possibly Milton, too. She has seen him turn strange and loud—when he wakens from a nightmare or a siren passes—unlike the silent man she married, but talking and ranting and shaking, strange clicking sounds between his words as if his teeth were chattering.

She decides to concentrate on how kind he is, how curious about the world, how sweet to his daughters when they are quiet. She will put her love for him on top of her thoughts, like the Bible instructs. She envisions a bed in a clean room, wallpaper with cabbage roses; the girls asleep in little cots. In her daydream, she takes down her hair and gives him her brush and lets the wonderful feeling of his love flow through his hand, through the soft stroking. After her hair and her heart have turned to silk, they lay on the bed and are husband and wife, normal and in love. She imagines this over and over, adding details—a dresser with a curved mirror, the smell of Milton's neck like corn mixed with soap, healthy, wholesome, the little curve of scar above his lip that she loves to kiss. She's sorry when Doris and Mildred wake. Now there is only time to be a mother.

It's past nine o'clock when the train slows for their station. For the past ten minutes, as dark turned the windows into mirrors, Doris has been patting her own reflection, saying, "Me, me, me." Now Edith whispers in her ear, "Who are we going to see?"

"Daddy, Daddy, my daddy."

"When you see him, run right to him and give him a big kiss." Doris gives her mother a worried look. "In case you don't remember him, I'll point to him so you know." A kind passenger helps them alight; Edith, holding Mildred, shoves the suitcase away from the hiss of the train with her foot; Doris stands on the platform, swinging her now-crumpled skirt. Edith glances at the station clock. They are so very late. She prays that Milton shows up, that he'll be calm and have found a nice quiet room. *Please, Lord.*

"Is that Daddy?"

Edith looks. "Of course it is. Go, you smart girl." Doris dashes down the platform and leaps at her father. He staggers but catches her; Edith sees how thin he is, but he's smiling his sweet smile and hugging Doris. Their child. Her husband. Gripping Mildred closer, she hurries toward him, holding out her free hand.

THEEEEEEETTTTTT! The train blasts a departing whistle.

Milton jumps as if shot and drops Doris. Although safely on

her feet, Doris's face bursts wide with fright and surprise. Edith wants to run to Milton but first she calls, "What a fun game. Can you jump as high as your daddy?" Doris's face closes into a smile and she begins hopping and singing, "I jump high, high, high."

A station manager passes with a sack of mail and Edith remembers they are in public; there will be no running. She walks to Milton and takes his hand. "Oh my dear. The train was so slow. I'm sorry."

"No, no, it's fine. Wonderful that you are here. I am. My . . . I am glad." He steps closer, almost huddling, as if she were a wall, a tree.

She touches his face. "Do we have a place to stay?"

"Oh, yes, I went everywhere. So many places not suited to women and children, but yes, a nice boarding house, a room of our own, breakfast included." The words stop. She can feel the trembling of his hand, see the little catches in his breath. Fie on custom, she wants to hold him close, but Mildred clings to her leg. "That sounds fine." She waits. He begins again. "Eggs, the woman said. Every morning. Healthy for children. And bacon and biscuits with gravy."

"Milton, that's wonderful. Can we go straight there? The girls need to sleep." The train is leaving the station and rather than shouting to be heard, she leans in until she catches the smell of his neck. She wants to lay her cheek on his. He passes his arm around her waist and presses close. Edith feels lonely and loved at the same time; she whispers, "We will sit together and talk quietly. You can brush my hair." A car passes the station and, remembering how exposed they are, she steps back. "Will we have time before you must return to the hospital?"

"No." His posture tightens. "Yes. Time." He looks at the large clock on the station wall: 9:45. "Well, I . . ." He steps closer into her protection—the clean smell of lemon—and looks into Mildred's little face. He smiles and she feels him relax. "You see, I don't have to go back. The doctor has given me an all-night pass."

Knowing they will be sleeping in the same bed, Edith feels a small thrill. He's thin and shaky, but Milton is her husband, the father to her children, and she loves him in many ways. Taking Doris by the hand and cradling Mildred, she waits for him to pick up the suitcase, then the family moves slowly out of the empty station into the summer evening.

NOVEMBER 1928, MILTON

A VOCATIONAL CENTER IN IOWA

The reed is smooth and brown. The glass is cool and clear. Underneath the glass, fabric lies in a clean oval, cut by Milton under the watchful eyes of the attendant who took back the scissors on the instant of the last snip. The fabric is flowered, chosen for Edith, with roses and daisies in her favorite color—blue.

Milton rests his hands on the glass and feels its clarity seep up his fingertips. The torn cuticle on his thumb becomes transparent. The little hairs on his wrist frost over like grass in an ice storm. In a minute, cool as an icebox, he will lift the smooth reed and braid it into the edge of the tray he is making. A gift. He imagines her stepping onto a porch, iced tea glasses rattling slightly. "Isn't it beautiful? My husband made it for me." He knows she would never betray him to scorn by adding, "He was in an institution."

He concentrates on the glass, which he buffs whenever a fingerprint mars the shine. The attendant sighs as Milton polishes;

the woman needs to learn patience. No need to hurry. I will be here for months.

Done with the polishing, he waits until his hands turn to glass again, then picks up a reed and begins pulling it through the hole he had drilled under the watchful eye of the attendant. He likes the way the reed bends but is also stiff, pressing against his fingers, firm and decided; the reed is like the man Milton wants to be. He concentrates on the brown, like the color of his own hair. He could be like the reed, yes, yes. He pulls another strand through the hole, using a little force, feeling strong and in control. This reed over, next one under, he knows the pattern, his hands begin to melt, the wrist hair soft and springing away from skin. He braids. The reed bends and holds.

"Occupational therapy will be over in ten minutes," the attendant announces.

Milton's hands begin to shake. He tries to continue weaving but a reed snaps in his fingers. He pushes the tray to one side and presses his hands onto his thighs, which are thin and shaky like the legs of a just-born colt. He sits on his trembling hands, willing them still as the fear crawls up his shins, up and up, through the knobs of his knees, the whorls of his gut, the rack of his ribs. Transparency gone, he fills with apple butter, fruit burnt in the iron kettle in his mother's backyard, a brown mush. Although he stares at the tray, at the blue fabric and empty glass, it has lost its magic. Because after therapy comes the chicken coop.

He is supposed to be learning how to farm chickens. To support his wife, his children. But he finds only horror in the coops: the cacophony and flapping. Feathers of Rhode Island Reds flying like drops of blood in slow motion, spattering his shirt, his pants. Like Herbert's blood on his uniform—no, no. Milton puts his forehead down on the table and shuts his eyes.

"Mr. Fieth?" The attendant knows not to touch him without warning. When she places her hand on his shoulder, he sees the pink skin and the clean fingernails, but there is no weight. Carefully he lifts his head.

"Do you want me to put your tray away?"

He nods, his throat filled with apple muck.

The therapist comes into the room. "Oh, Mr. Fieth, such a beautiful tray. Your wife is going to be so pleased." He steps across to the table.

Milton looks away; he can hear mechanical gears turn in his neck. The brown fear is gagging him. "Mr. Fieth?" Milton puts his head down. "You mustn't skip your course work again." The therapist sits down, reaches across the table and places a hand on Milton's hair. "Think of your wife and your beautiful daughters. They need you. And you want to support them like a husband and father would. I know you do." The therapist pats Milton. "Come on, son, let's go together."

Milton trembles and jerks but is unable to rise; the therapist sighs and leaves the room.

DECEMBER 1928, EDITH

KNOXVILLE, IOWA

Edith lays down the book *Standard Poultry Production*. Farming chickens isn't as easy as she thought. Her mother kept a few and as a child it had been her job to gather the still-warm eggs, hens ruffling and pecking around her knees, the little coop like an exploded feather bed. She had hated the smears of chicken dung on the shells and it ruined her taste for eggs, but when a chicken was killed for dinner, her mother dried the plucked feathers and put them into a feed sack, saving them for pillows. Edith loved stirring through that sack, looking for treasures—a reddish feather with white polka dots hidden among pale yellow, white, brown, striped. There were duck feathers mixed in, iridescent with crunchy spines. But now that Milton is studying chicken farming at the vocational center, Edith knows poultry means business and she'll have to learn as much or more as he does because she'll be the one taking care of the hens. She breathes through her dismay and thanks the Lord for bringing them to safety after Milton was kicked out of the Jefferson Barracks. She knows for him, their night together was worth the poverty and humiliation. And now, as long as he studies at the center, the government will pay for him to learn. Such a relief. She can pay the bills and the girls can eat.

She pages through the book, pausing at pictures of single hens and little speckled flocks. Toward the back, there are sample chicken houses that look as if they require expertise in carpentering. When Milton leaves the school and the stipend stops, how on earth will they afford carpentry? And how to pay for the stock? She calculates the cost of feed per chicken and writes the figures in a column. So much money. She must learn quickly; her girls are growing. They need to eat well. She pauses to say a short prayer—*Lord please help us. Milton needs you. We need him. But thank you for letting us be together, not like in the last hospital.* Here, although Milton has to stay on the school grounds, the doctor allows her to visit weekly and the family has one day a month together.

Enough of chickens! Turning the page, she starts a shopping list: five pounds of flour, yeast for bread, two pounds rice, bacon, beans, lard, Postum, milk. She crosses out bacon and Postum, writing DOLLS. Enough of the budget! The girls won't remember weeks of eating only beans, but they will remember the Christmas they got their dollies.

She takes off her apron and puts on a tweed coat. Wondering briefly if the shopkeeper will be scandalized if she doesn't wear a hat, she steps outside to find the late November cold; she returns for her scarf. Simpler. No hatpin required. As she cuts through the gas station on the corner, a kid at the red pump hollers, "Morning Missus Fieth." The little pipsqueak; yesterday her girls said he called their father a loony. She was horrified. "You must ignore such gossip. You're both old enough to understand it's not true. I don't want to hear such talk again." Now she nods briefly at the kid, puts her hand to her mouth, holding back her words with the rough wool of her glove, and walks quickly past.

In the thirteen blocks to the square, every person she passes greets her by name, including two little boys ducking and mumbling—caught playing hooky by Miz Fieth who knows their mothers from church. This is a town of Methodists, who meet at Sunday and Wednesday services, at funerals, baptisms, and the twice-yearly bazaars for which Edith has donated crocheted baby booties which don't take much yarn but plainly demonstrate her love of God and support of her fellow believers.

At the grocer's, she buys two onions, a quarter pound of beans, a pound of potatoes, and a quart of milk, picking carefully through the glass bottles until she sees a thin skim of yellow cream at the top; more nourishment for her girls. She considers buying an expensive orange but no, the dried apples in her cupboard will suffice. Putting the paper-wrapped purchases in her coat pockets and the milk bottle in a string bag, she thanks the grocer and hurries through the wind to the dry goods store.

Displayed in the window are long-legged dolls with little bow lips, eyes that open and close, and hair in swirls around their molded faces; the one in yellow is for Doris; Mildred's is in pink. Edith is sorry that her girls have outgrown the Raggedy Ann and Andy she made; she had such fun stitching up the dress and the overalls, sewing red yarn hair, making eyes out of shoe buttons from discarded boots. Those well-loved dolls are now tattered, loops of hair pulled loose, black-cloth feet graying. It's time for new dolls, but not baby dolls, since as Doris says, "We're too old."

Inside the store, windows are sealed and the room well heated; Mr. Hamilton, the proprietor, keeps the stove in the basement fired hot all day. Comprised of a single big room lined with floor-to-ceiling shelves, the store has a distinctive smell: hot air rising through brass grates heats the stock so that the principal scent is of fabric, the smell of ironing. Mixed in is licorice from the Black Jack gum Mr. Hamilton keeps by the cash register and the faint odor of shoe polish; his shoes are black mirrors peeping out from his suit pants.

"Good day, Mrs. Fieth." Another Methodist. He leans across the glass counter; under his elbow, a rainbow of ties. "How can I help you?"

"I'd like to purchase two dolls."

He comes out from behind the counter, goes to the window and picks up one in pink and one in yellow.

"How do you know I want those?"

"I seen the little girlies standing right out front there after school most days, pointing and sighing. These are for yours."

Edith smiles as she imagines this balding bachelor paying attention to a gaggle of small girls and vows to ask him to supper as a kindness. She hopes he eats beans.

"Do you require anything more?"

"I'll be needing some yarn and bits of fabric." She plans to knit and sew wardrobes for the dolls, all the nice clothes she can't afford to provide for her daughters. She spends twenty-three cents more than she intended because at the last minute Mr. Hamilton shows her some red velvet, just in and perfect for Christmas. She envisions vests for the girls, not as expensive as jackets, but sweet and festive.

More beans, she thinks as she steps into the street. The clock in the Lutheran church tower—the town has a few dissidents—strikes one o'clock. Edith hurries home to hide the dolls, to read more about chickens, and to prepare their supper: rice with onions fried in bacon fat, a jar of the tomatoes she stewed in the summer, and dried apples in a crisp.

The crisp is in the oven when the little house bounces as the girls hit the front steps and Doris bursts in, crying, "Mother, Mother!" Her scarf has slipped off her dark hair and her mittens dangle from the crocheted chain Edith made after two pairs went missing in a month.

"Oh Mommy." Mildred's close behind, her hair still combed and her shoelaces in neat bows, but the crescents of her smiling eyes flattened with worry.

Doris starts again, "Let me tell."

"You said I could. Mommy!"

"You'll tell it wrong." Doris pushes Mildred aside.

"No fair." Mildred tugs Doris's scarf.

"Keep it up and you'll both go to your room and I'll hear nothing," says Edith.

"Okay, cry baby Mildred, you tell." Doris pulls off her coat and flings it to the floor.

"Hang that up please, young lady."

"Oh Mommy," Mildred begins, then starts to wail. "Someone. . ." wah, wah, "the dolls. . ." waaah, "after school."

"You can't tell it right. Let me." Doris picks up her coat and tosses it over Mildred's head. "The dolls are gone from the store window. Our special dolls." She stomps her foot.

Mildred pushes the coat back to the floor. "We wanted them sooooo much."

"Someone stole them," says Doris.

"Are you sure?"

"Mr. Hamilton said so."

Edith keeps from laughing. "You mustn't bother Mr. Hamilton. He's busy."

"But our dolls."

"These things happen. You'll live. Doris, hang up your coat!" She clears a space on the table. "Do you have homework?"

"Mildred has a spelling test." Doris sticks her tongue out at her sister.

"Let her tell me, sweetie. Mildred?"

"Big words." Mildred plops into a chair. "I'll never use them."

"Wait until you get to second grade like me. Then you will." Doris puffs out her chest. "I know ever so many big words."

"And I have to write sentences." Mildred leans her head on the table.

"Well," Edith pulls out a chair, "you'd better start."

Doris picks up the chicken book on the table. "Can I look at the picture for just a minute?" She's enamored of chicken transport. Edith knows her daughter once visited the train station to ask if any chicken trains were expected.

In a chapter about getting products to market, there's a picture of a long train car outfitted like an apartment house for birds. Eight rows of cages stacked seven high. The caption says each car holds about 4,600 chickens and is *equipped with a water tank, grain crib and a room for an attendant who cares for the birds. Eggs laid on route are the property of the crew.* Two satisfied men loll on top of the car. Doris kneels on the chair, crouching over the book, tracing the little squares of the cages. "Sit like a lady, please," says Edith. She chuckles inside remembering the conversation with the station master as they exited church. She loves Doris's imagination.

When their homework is done, they say grace, eat, wash and put away dishes, then play with the pickup sticks their Granny sent for their birthdays earlier in the fall. When it's bedtime, Edith tucks them in. "Say your prayers," she says, just like every mother in town, whether Methodist, Lutheran, or the occasional Catholic. As she's leaving the room, Doris asks, "Mother, do you think Daddy will talk to us next time?"

The words make Edith lean on the door. "Sweetie, let's hope he will. He's sick but he loves you."

"I know. I pray for him twice—between Granny and Bampa, then between you and Mildred."

Edith takes off her glasses and rubs them on her apron. "That's nice." She goes back to kiss the girls again. "Sleep tight." The ancient gesture of pulling up the covers, tucking, smoothing hair. As she's leaving, Doris says, "Sing a song, Mother."

"Yes, yes, pretty please," says Mildred.

"With sugar on it."

Edith's heart hurts and she doesn't feel like singing, but these are her daughters. For them she will push down her sorrows and make a normal life. "*Baby's fishing for a dream, fishing near and far.*"

"We fished at Granny's."

"Shhh, go to sleep. *His line a golden moonbeam is.*"

"*Her*, Mother. We're girls."

"*Her bait a silver star.*"

Doris turns over, slinging her arm across Mildred. They go to sleep like this every night.

"*Sail baby sail.*" Edith is edging out the door. "*Out upon the sea. Only don't forget to sail back again to me.*" She pulls the door shut.

At the table she cleans her glasses and picks up the chicken book again. It's true Milton isn't talking. She had planned a surprise for the November visit—a birthday party—Doris being seven in November and Mildred six in early December. She made two little cakes decorated with one of the candles she uses after the girls are in bed (they need electricity to save their eyes; she needs candles to save on their bills). Also in her basket were bright homemade birthday cards, a handful of penny candy as much for Milton's sweet tooth as for the girls, and a mason jar wrapped in a towel with coffee made the way he liked it: boiled and strong.

The day had been a failure.

One of the nurses, seeing Edith holding Milton's hand, the two little girls fidgeting in the cloud of silence, and the cakes on the table, hurried over, smiling, and asked, "Whose birthday?" She brought out a soda bottle for the "birthday girls" to share and then asked if they would like their picture taken with their daddy.

Edith was too stunned by her mute husband, by the dread she felt as he sat hanging his head like a condemned man, by the girls' attempts to talk to him; she neither protested nor protected but followed the nurse out to the porch—"This old camera needs lots of light"—and standing behind her family, let the nurse take the picture.

When Edith returned alone for her next visit, the nurse sought her out.

"He's having a hard time." She handed Edith the picture. "He's going to need a lot of help when you start the farm." She slipped a book into Edith's large purse. "We want to help him; on a good day, he's a charming man. And your family seems . . ." The nurse pauses. "Well, let me know if I can do anything."

Now, in her little rickety house, Edith reads the chicken book.

Beginners are urged to keep but one variety of a breed of fowls.

While Edith's dream of having a sack full of various feathers fades, she consciously thinks she never should have allowed the girls to see their daddy like that.

The question is frequently asked, "Which is the best breed of fowls?"

It's hard enough for her. If Milton is going to pass this training, she must help him more. In the summer she'll send the girls away to his folks in Warrenton or her own family in Enterprise. Concentrate on his needs.

She flips past several pictures, then carries a candle over to look into the girls' room. They are sleeping, curled back to back now. She settles the thin quilt over them, wondering if she should write to her mother and ask for feathers; with feathers she could make a warm comforter. Although she has traded her own baking for extra wood, the little house is cold in the corners, damp in the middle, and in the mornings the floor is icy.

Her mother didn't approve of her marriage although she's never said so directly. "Are you sure, dear?" was her only comment when Edith told her Milton would be asking for her hand in marriage. Edith wanted to say, "Enterprise is small, the men few. Here is my chance, maybe the last one; he loves me despite my nose." Instead, she only said, "I can make him happy. Then he'll settle down."

"I hope so for your sake."

"I love him, Mother. Won't that make a difference?"

"Yes, but he was in the Great War. That will also make a difference in his life. And yours."

"Love will make the biggest difference."

“Perhaps you are right. With love and with God, all things are possible.”

Suddenly Edith wishes for her mother’s warm arms, for her family’s house, the smell of chicken cooking, potatoes, beans and peas on the table, the green gravy boat, the hiss of the gas lamp in the hall and the murmurs on the porch that mean her parents were resting before the meal and talking over their day. Oh Mother. How she misses her.

The White Wyandotte finds favor on many farms as a desirable producer of eggs.

Edith tells herself not to cry, to be strong. She made this family with God’s help. She will keep it together with His help. She reads on.

AUGUST 1930, MILTON

OSCEOLA, IOWA

Although he loves the freedom of walking purposefully by himself, Milton avoids crowds, keeping close to the store windows, ducking into an alley when a gaggle of boys in baseball uniforms jostles down the sidewalk. Crowds tend to bursts of laughter, dropped packages, squeals of delight. Noise makes him panic; suddenness makes him run. That is why he failed at chicken farming: broody hens flapping up from their perches, roosters crowing behind his back. As he waits for the boys to pass, he stares down the alley at the trash and piles of boxes, pushing down the memory like Dr. E. advised. After all, the chicken failure was over a year ago. Now he lives in Paso, Iowa, and like a regular man with a family, runs a country store where he sells salt, tuna, sugar, and mason jars to local farmers. Because the store is set in the middle of the fields—convenient for farmers' wives—there are no frightening noises and he has calmed down.

The boys pass. He exits the alley and is scuttling down the sidewalk when women swarm out of Woolworth's, talking loudly, their heels pounding dull staccato. Braced, Milton focuses on the shop window: a pyramid of thread, a stack of cotton fabric, little packets of needles. Perhaps he should buy something for his wife. She loves to sew. No, he must save his money because last time there was a mistake. He will earn Edith's trust, be like any husband, in charge, walking away from the thread, knowing how much he can spend.

The sidewalk empties and he can walk faster. Calm and trusted. He knows where he left the car. Reliable and in charge. He knows where he is going: 354 Wilson. Edith mailed a list to the supply house and they are expecting him. He will simply walk in the door, pay, and carry the packages to the car.

As he turns the corner onto Wilson, he notices a set of dishes displayed in a shop window. Ivory with delicate flowers around the rim—china for company. He stops, feels the delight of the flowers and the shiny porcelain, clear and polished, not a single fingerprint. Just the thing farmers' wives will appreciate. French-looking. Special to display in the case under the cash register in his store. Yes, he should buy them. In honor of the Frenchies who died. And ... his mind stutters, blackens, then he pushes down Herbert, Oberly, Socks. *Concentrate on the flowers.* After a moment he is able to reach through his dark thoughts and open the door. He manages not to flinch at the bell or the swish of the fan. A young man, jacket removed against the heat, walks down a row of shelves, wielding a feather duster. In the corner a mop leans in a bucket; the shop smells of yellow soap.

"How much for the dishes?" Milton gestures to the window.

The quoted price is more than he has in cash—Edith gives him only enough for gas, supper, and a piece of pie at the diner. He has a moment's pause. Will she be angry? He is sure he can sell the dishes for a profit, seeing as they come from the big city. A sales pitch runs in his head: *Just that special touch for your Sunday supper with visiting relatives.* A farmer's wife smiles at him, says, *How did you know my in-laws are coming?* and takes money from her pocketbook. Yes, he will buy the dishes. Looking the clerk in the eye, Milton smiles. "How about we do a deal?"

The clerk turns away, polishing a glass counter with his cuff; he's a young fella, never been to war—the hair on Milton's arm rises—has a wedding ring; probably struggling to feed his family. Milton knows how that feels. Calm and in control. "Say, you got kids?" He leans on the glass, careful not to smudge it. "Me, I got two daughters. A year apart. Beautiful little girls."

"Mine's a son." The words begrudging, but it's hot and there are no other customers.

"I'll bet he's a fine lad. He like watermelon or apples? Or maybe he goes for candy."

"He's two."

"Ah." Does a two-year-old have teeth yet? A moment's panic; he can't remember his girls when they were two. What did they look like? What did they wear and say? Those years are gone. He pushes the worry down. "Anyway, about this deal. I want those dishes. I see they're special-like." He decides to forego supper, saving just enough for pie. "How-some-ever, I don't have the money, but what say I give you half in dollars and pay for the rest in canned goods. Or sugar. Or flour. You name it. Even jam. Take some home to your wife and son."

Milton leaves the shop, grinning. His gift of gab serves him well in business, yes indeedy. Half an hour later he has the dishes in the car with the rest of the stock, only short a bunch of bananas, a pound of sugar, and two tins of lard. Sitting on the hot fender of the little car, he counts his money; enough for pie but down the street is a moving picture house. He could see a show, sleep in the car, and drive back to Paso tomorrow. No worries; Edith knows he can take care of himself. He is out on the street, a man doing a man's business, providing for his family. Standing, he settles his hat. She is going to love the dishes, be proud of him. Flour, salt, canned tuna—his customers buy those every day of their lives—but dishes with hopeful pink roses that twinkle around the edges! Special. Make one smile at dinner. Maybe Edith will want them herself. He'll bring them into the house and she'll be so happy that he thought of her.

He smiles, hands in his pocket as he walks toward the theater; he hopes the movie is funny. If not, he'll just get himself some pie. Cherry. With a scoop of ice cream. A man about his business.

AUGUST 1930, EDITH

PASO, IOWA

The morning is prairie-quiet. When Edith steps out onto the porch she is totally alone, surrounded by endless fields through which a dirt road meanders, no neighbor to be seen, her only company a raptor floating in the sky, ends of its wings spread like fingers to catch the rising air. She imagines herself Dorothy in Oz but caught in fields of corn, not poppies. No Emerald City, no wizard, no balloon waiting to fly her away. Just the endless work of the store. Worries night and day. Although Milton has stopped screaming, no longer frightening the girls in the night, they pay for his calm by living like hermits. Stuck out here without their families, with the dust, the heat, the endless sun ... *My, I got up on the wrong side of the bed this morning.* She gives thanks that they have a house and food, unlike the wanderers she sees suffering from the Great Crash.

While summer stokes its furnace and the corn stalks chitter in a small wind, she squints down the road, expecting to see the family car, but the dry grass by the store is empty. She had hoped

Milton arrived late and, rather than wake the girls, slept outside. Wherever is he? Has he been scared by some sound? The last time that happened—a bugle frightened him on the Fourth of July—he was gone for hours. Her father finally found him by the river and led him home, muddy and confused.

At least there's no windmill in the nearby fields. If he jumped again and died, would she be better off? Is a dead husband better than a crazy one? *Don't think that.* But she could live in Enterprise, drink tea with Hortense on a civilized porch, close to her family with the girls . . . *no, no! Forgive me Lord. Bring him safely home to us. His daughters need him. And so do I.*

She stands on the porch praying until the ugly spasm passes and she can concentrate on her other problem: Malinda, Milton's sister, arrives today for a visit from Warrenton. The train station is thirteen miles away and Milton has the car. If Malinda is left waiting at the station she might return home, and Edith needs this visit. She opens and closes the ragged screen, staring out at the hard blue sky. *I know you're up there. Help me figure this out.*

An engine coughs awake out of sight over the hill. Her nearest neighbors, the Hatschenbachers, are going to market with their eggs. Doris and Mildred, young ears alert, come running out onto the splintery porch, barefoot, in frayed cotton nightgowns.

When the Hatschenbachers crest the hill in their flivver, the girls begin to wave. Down they come, the mister hanging grimly onto the wheel, looking as if the car is driving him, the missus's bonnet ribbons blowing back. She lifts the basket of eggs off her lap in preparation for the leap the car makes over the little creek. *Whoosh*, the girls excitedly wave the car into the air, *thump*, it lands; the eggs survive. Life in danger, Edith steps out onto the edge of the road and holds up her hands. Squealing like a resentful animal, the little vehicle stops. Ghosts of dust float up as Edith arranges Malinda's ride.

Edith prays *Please let the train run on time* and goes into the house to make breakfast. The store is supposed to open at 8 a.m.; without Milton's help, she's going to have to rush to get the girls fed and settled for the day.

"Where's Daddy?" Mildred's a Daddy's girl.

"Still on his trip. Getting supplies for the store." Edith fears that's not all he's doing. The last trip was not a success; he broke the sack of sugar on some stray tools in the car and, distracted by a conversation with a stranger, left one whole box of provisions on the side of the road. She hopes some poverty-stricken wanderer found it and had solid meals for several days, but because of this disaster, she has been forced to tell customers that there are no cans of tuna or beans—not so bad, she still has canned salmon and garden vines will soon yield beans—but worse than the missing cans, both sugar and salt have run low. It's almost canning season; gardens are full, trees bend with ripe fruit. In fact, she's planning a peach pie for dinner. She says to herself what she has been saying to her customers all week, "I do believe brown sugar will serve." The shame of those words makes her feel the tightness of her girdle and the points of her hairpins.

“Stiiiiilll on that stupid trip?” Doris thumps her book on the table and wiggles into the blouse Edith made for her at the beginning of the summer, yellow checked with a ruffle. “When’s he coming home?”

“Soon. We all miss him.” Edith tries to make her voice even as she pours pancake batter into the skillet.

“If Daddy’s not here, can I open the store?” Mildred—in matching blue checks, younger but ever more responsible—stands up from the table.

“Eat your pancakes honey. If we hear a car or horse, then yes, I’d appreciate your help. Doris, I need you to pick some peaches. Your Aunt Malinda is coming today, and I’m going to make a pie.” Edith knows that Malinda will ease her worries; all of Milton’s family have been ever so kind about Milton’s troubles, but his sister is Edith’s favorite. For one thing, Malinda has a job, like Edith has a job. And she’s older than Milton, a big sister worrying for him along with Edith. And finally, she has a mind of her own, which gives Edith hope.

When the Hatschenbachers drop Malinda off, Edith is just placing the pie on the windowsill to cool. She gives them a dollar’s worth of gas in thanks for Malinda’s lift; the girls chatter and pull their aunt around their little domain. “Here’s the store,” they point. “There’s the feed shop. We have pigs and a cow and we get to feed them. Daddy’s going to teach us how to milk. Up there is the creek and that’s the Andy Hall, where the horse thieves have their rituals.”

Soon the girls return to their summer pursuits, and the two

women settle in the store, ice chips piled in the tea glasses. "I'm not expecting any customers. Mr. Larson came yesterday for feed. He asked about having his horse shod, but he had to wait."

"You don't shoe horses yourself?" Malinda laughs a little.

"Heavens no. You should see his horse, though. A beautiful roan with a fine arched neck and lashes. You know how I love the lashes on a horse."

"I do know." Malinda pulls a fan from her pocket, polite because the electric fan in the corner looks broken. "How are you liking it way out here? Do you have neighbors?"

"There's the old couple that brought you. They live over the hill. Mostly it's quiet, which is good in a way. No one gossips about us. Milton's calmer."

"He's such a talker, though. Does he miss what he calls his gab?"

"He can bend the customers' ears, so I guess not."

"I gather he's not here."

Trusting Malinda to be close-mouthed, Edith tells of her husband's frights and of her struggles with the army and their denial of Milton's insurance claim. "They say his problems don't come from the war and they won't pay." She should push the tears down, but when Malinda pats her hand, she cries.

Malinda in turn cries as she tells about her fiancé to whom she has been engaged for seven years; they can't marry because his mother is poorly and as the only son, he must care for her. "He's getting gray and worn from worry," she says, "and I am getting gray from waiting." Edith assures her that she's as lovely as ever (the Fieth girls are as beautiful as the boys are handsome) and the talk moves on to happier topics.

"Last week I found the girls dipping the feet of their dolls into the creek and wiping the water off with their own hair."

"What in heaven's name?"

"They were playing 'washing the feet of Jesus.' Something they heard about in Sunday school." Edith hopes this isn't blasphemy.

"They told me about the Andy Hall and the horse thief. Ante hall?"

"Correct. Doris won't go near the place; she insists that a horse thief died in there, his ghost is going to get her and that the sawhorses are used in some sort of ritual. Did you ever hear the like?"

"Sawhorses?"

"We keep them as table legs for oyster suppers. Only time the local women get out to socialize, except for church doings. The men are often in there though, using some excuse or another to drink and spit and talk."

"And Milton in the thick, gabbing."

"He prefers his conversations one at a time. And those men, they do get loud, which affects his nerves terribly." Edith turns on the fan that squeals as one of the local women enters to buy a pound of lard. "Hot weather for frying," she comments when the woman is gone. She turns off the fan and says loudly in the sudden silence, "I want to ask you something." She speaks softer. "You work with those veterans of the Civil War. Any of them twitch or behave like Milton?"

"I had thought to watch but haven't noticed any such behavior. I asked the doctor and he said that although 'soldier's heart' occurred during the Civil War, shell shock was different. Solely a result of the Great War, of men losing their nerve, fleeing from the battle. Made me mighty angry."

A horse and wagon passes on the road outside; Edith closes the door against the dust.

"When I asked the director, he had another idea. He said in the War Between the States battles lasted a short, bloody time, two days at most, then the armies disengaged and cleaned up. Those fellows in Germany were bombarded for weeks. Unrelenting bombs and noise, he said. Friends dying around them, tanks, artillery. Not what our Civil War veterans experienced, and it was more devastating, he presumed. I reckon he was right. I once asked Mr. Enright, one of our guests, what he remembered from his war and he said, 'Blood, mud, and marching. Them generals didn't give a rat's whisker for our feet. I was blamed-near killed by the marching.'"

The women drink their tea in silence. Up the hill, they can hear the little girls splashing in the creek. "It's so hot the corn might just pop right off the stalks," says Malinda. "Let's sit out with the girls. You can see the store from there, can you not?"

It's a leisurely afternoon and the sun is going down when they head back toward the house. Suddenly Doris yells and starts to run. "Look, look!"

The Hatschenbachers' cat is sitting on the peach pie, nibbling. As Doris runs wildly toward the house, the cat springs away. She snatches the pie off the windowsill.

"Enough left for our dinner," Edith says and takes the pie inside to cut away the little teeth marks. As she's setting out plates, Mildred and Doris begin calling, "Daddy's home. Daddy's home." *Thank you Lord.*

It's a gay supper. Milton recounts his adventures. "Got us a real good deal, Edith. Traded some of the foodstuffs for a set of dishes. They'll sell right fine, I'm betting. Farmers' wives like that kind of thing."

Please don't let him have traded away the salt or the sugar. "We'll have fun unpacking the car tomorrow, won't we girls?" Edith says. "What else did you do?"

"Went to a moving picture called *The Big City*. The piano player was real good. Made you feel every idea those actors had in their heads. I'd like to see one of them new talking pictures, but I'm not sure I'll like it."

"I want to see one, Daddy!"

"I'll take you all sometime." He gestures around the table.

Edith clears the plates and brings out the pie, glad there is no movie theater nearby; tickets are bound to be expensive.

"Seems like someone's had a piece of that pie already," Milton says.

"It was the caaaat!" Mildred bests her sister in announcing the event.

Milton watches Edith cut the pie. "Don't be giving me a slice from where the cat ate. Might be some stray whiskers." He lifts an eyebrow at his daughters and grins. "Don't give it to Malinda or the girls, neither." He pats his wife's hand. "Honey, looks like you're going to get that slice."

Edith smiles at him. She loves his teasing.

"The nibbled crust is trimmed away, Miltie," says Malinda.

"Uh huh." He digs into his piece. "Poor Edith. Having to eat where the cat munched. Bits of fur tucked into the peaches."

"No, Daddy, Mother cut it off real good."

"Tickle your throat, honey." Milton's in high spirits, flourishing his fork, winking at the girls, patting Edith's leg under the table. "The cat's snack piece."

Edith starts to laugh; this is the Milton she fell in love with. "Yes, I am eating that slice, but my dear, you are eating the piece where the cat sat."

DECEMBER 1933, MILTON

ENTERPRISE, KANSAS

Milton's afraid to fall asleep—the dreams! Herbert spurting blood from his ears and neck, Socks running barefoot over barbed wire, leaving a trail of red; the black figures coming closer until darkness shuts down his eyes, but yes, he can still hear: Edith in the kitchen, sending the girls off to school, words like echoes in a cave. He tries to hold their voices, but wind batters the window, a tornado of sound; he mustn't go deaf, he needs to hear his family. The wind begins to sing nasty songs, songs of evil and death and marching. "This is it. The real thing." And over the wall into death. He wants to cover his ears, to drown his fright as Dr. E. said, but his arms are no longer his; they are blown off, laying in a field, palms broken into blood by his fingernails. His failures! Anvils in his life, no chickens, no store, everything lost. He struggles to rise, longs to eat, to work, to be a man, husband, father. He cannot move, legs rigid, far away, sticks attached to feet; his toes quiver and disappear; he sweats with the effort to bring them back. How will he stand without toes? Sock's feet reappear, running over black dirt, filthy, toenails torn away. Milton cannot push the thought down. It bobs in his mind, is joined by Herbert laughing clots of black blood, by Oberly inhaling mud and clawing. Suddenly Milton is angry, red hot instead of frozen, words that shouldn't be spoken streaming through him—*god damn damn damn damn damn god damn to hell war bombs death*—the words are a volcano; they spurt out his mouth, run down his face, burn his cheeks, his chin, his neck. The bedclothes catch fire. Edith runs into the room and grabs his thin shoulder as he screams and screams.

APRIL 1934, EDITH

ENTERPRISE, KANSAS, AND KANSAS CITY, MISSOURI

Edith's mother sets a basket on the table; it contains five eggs, a couple of onions, jars of canned peaches, a soup-can filled with rice, a quart of milk, and a loaf of fresh-made bread.

"Mother, I . . ." Edith stops. In her little pantry a pound of beans, sent to her by Malinda, and some flour. No apples, not a single potato, no sugar, no lard. There has been no butter for weeks.

"It's okay, dear. Your girls are growing. That scamp Doris is all legs and wrists." She pats Edith softly on the arm. "My granddaughters are among the smart ones, or so I heard the teacher saying yesterday at the post office."

Edith knows they are smart—Doris reads constantly and uses words like obnoxious and exuberant; Mildred likes to help with the weekly accounts. Milton may be damaged, but his girls are not and she's glad her mother knows it.

"Sit a while? I can make tea." Tea she has, thanks to Milton's brother, and the cups are free of stains because she used salt and vinegar on them just this morning. A year ago when the store in Iowa failed, her mother offered the old house, rent free, and Edith wants to keep it up like she's been taught—dusting, washing, polishing, airing the bedclothes, honoring her mother's gift. She feels safe in its comfort, despite the cranky furnace in the basement and the tilted back porch steps, and wants to give the girls a real home, a house where they can root and grow into their lives. "There's no sugar," Edith says to her mother.

"No thanks, sweetie. I have bread in the oven." As she goes out the door, she adds, "I'm slaughtering chickens this afternoon. We've got extra. Your father will bring one over." She's gone before Edith can protest.

Edith lays her head down; the twisting grain of the old wood table like so many roads doesn't soothe her as usual. Nothing soothes her. Milton in the Kansas City hospital, her cupboards bare as the nursery rhyme, her daughters' breakfast, lunch, and dinner available only because of her in-laws and her family. She must find money. They will have to move to a city where she can get a job; she will learn to type, she has an education.

Her mother steps onto the back porch and calls out, "There's tornados predicted. Best get your laundry in." Then she's gone again.

Outside, the wind snaps the clothes on the line as Edith unpins dresses and slips, breathing in the sun-scented cotton, ignoring the frayed hems. Folding, ironing, setting to rights, her thoughts churn and churn. What to do? What to do? Like the sky, her mind is dark, lowering.

Chores done, she fetches the stack of official government papers from her bedside table. They're stored in an old candy box, heavy with questions and personal grief. The top-most recent letter is addressed to "Edith Fieth, Guardian." The last word presses her. Guardians are men. Guardians are for helpless widows or orphans. The world is surely topsy-turvy when she is *Guardian* of her husband. She has told no one in town about the paper; the humiliation to Milton would be too great if—no, *when*—he gets better and comes home. Soon, she hopes; the girls need their father. He's been away six months already, but the doctor says these cases take time and she must be patient. She sighs and pulls out a stack of pictures to search for her favorite.

The back porch stairs creak. "Hidee-ho, it's me."

She slides the box to cover the papers. "My dear! Come in. I didn't know you were back." Edith's friend Hortense and her husband Clarence have just returned from visiting New York. "Would you like a cup of tea?"

"Of course, you know me, glad to partake of homey rituals." Hortense sits and reaches across the table to the photos. "What's this?" The tea kettle squeals, Edith turns quickly, but too late. Hortense is holding a snapshot of men crowded on the deck of a ship. "I believe it's our men off to war. So fresh and cheerful and young, not yet bamboozled by the horrors of battle. Why ever do you have such a thing?"

Edith forces a smile. Sets down a cup for her friend who holds a photo of Milton sitting among men, smiling, the center of everything. "Look carefully."

Hortense holds the picture close to her eyes. "My goodness gracious, is that your husband?"

Edith pours tea from the dented pot and slides the cup over to Hortense. "On the *Antigone*, going to France." Edith knows her friend likes sweet tea but is certain she won't ask if it's not offered.

"He looks like a veritable king. So cocky. And such wonderful hair. Clarence is growing quite bald. I hope you don't mind my looking. You know I care immensely for you and your family. And these are so interesting, so informative."

It's true. Hortense has been among those who have helped, sending lengths of cotton for the girls' school clothes from her husband's mercantile store. Edith turns away as Hortense picks up a picture marked Bellevue Photographic Department; Milton stands stiffly with another man in front of a heavy building.

"Oh my dear. Such a difference in the man. We never realized when we first met him, did we? He was so lovely." Hortense grimaces slightly. "Is. . . .will be." She lays down the pictures and takes a sip of tea. "Delicious. Just what I needed."

Feeling he'll never be like that again, Edith places the photos in the box. "How was your trip? Such a long train ride."

"Oh my dear, completely stupendous. We ate in a French restaurant that had an absolutely exquisite fountain and acres of windows. They do go overboard in many things—eating snails, quite unimaginable—but their fashion sense is not to be denied. What I saw in the grand department stores. Such ravishing gowns and lingerie and hats and perfume. It was quite overwhelming. But I declare, too much walking required. My feet positively suffered."

Edith sips weak tea. "Your dress is new, isn't it? So pretty. I should have commented first off."

"Oh my, you are too delicious for noticing. It's a Chanel." She stands and twirls, the pleats flip and bobble. "Her nipped-in waists suit me perfectly." Hortense runs her hands from her ribs to her hips.

"Your figure is enviable." Edith has remained as she ever was: tall and stout.

When Hortense leaves to pay other visits—"You must come round for a dinner. Bring the girls, I'll tell them about the Empire State Building"—Edith imagines the fancy buildings, the lights, the water diverted for the fountains. The city must have a great many dollars, even though dollars are still in short supply because of the Crash. If money can be found for a tall building, why not for Milton? He was in the Great War. That's why he is ruined and she has become his Guardian.

Suddenly angry, she begins separating the papers, slapping down those that offered compensation and those that denied her claims. Here's the paper on which a doctor wrote that Milton had tachycardia, that his illness has nothing to do with the war. As if he hadn't done his duty; as if he wasn't brave. The doctor was a coward, calling Milton a shirker, a faker; he'd never been to war himself. He was like all the healthy young men in white shirts and ties, ignorant of Milton's suffering as he shrank pound by pound, untempted by the sweets he had so loved; they'd not heard him shouting in the night and seen his inability to go to town during the day, ashamed but unable to control the shivering and jerking when he walked. The damn war. Edith catches her breath. *Forgive me, Lord, but you know it isn't fair. Please heal Milton and bring him back to us. Amen.*

Most of the paperwork is for adjustments, how much should be paid for children and a wife, dollar amounts amortized over three months or two years or however long the government had ignored her pleas for money owed. As she reads, her hands cramp with anger. She imagines storming into an office, shaking the bureaucrats, spattering them with ink from their fancy pens. They are terrible at math, making her write again and again and pay postage she cannot afford, to get what is legally hers. Legally Milton's.

She holds for a moment the paper that causes her the most regret: regulations allow payment only one year prior to the date a claim is made. Five years of money lost because Milton refused to apply. Edith knows he refused because applying meant admitting that he wasn't getting better. He so wanted to be cheerful, to be sane and with his family.

She thinks of him on the windmill. The sunny day, the wild wind. If he had landed differently ... *Thank you Lord for saving him with a broken ankle.* She pushes down the memory of February, him screaming in the bedroom, then strapped onto the stretcher and taken to the train's baggage car. *Thank you Lord for our doctor, willing to ride all the way to Kansas City. Bring blessings to his family.* Hoping to ease the pressure she feels behind her eyes, on her shoulders, her heart, she finishes the bit of tea Hortense left in the cup.

The last paper before the one declaring her Guardian states: "The September payment at $90 will be final as your disability has been rated as less than 10%." Since then, there has been no money, the doctor and hospital bills are mounting, and Milton, far away from the support of his family, still suffers. She has been to Kansas City once where she saw him lying in the hospital bed, shaking and silent as at the birthday party in Iowa. Although she hated the screaming and cursing, silence was worse; it meant he was holding all his suffering inside.

Edith stands suddenly. Only she could help her—no, *their*—daughters. Why had she hesitated? She'd make them pay, all those bureaucrats with their fine cufflinks. They will give her money, nothing beyond what she is owed, but fair, she will demand fair. *Dear Lord, give me courage.* She puts on her hat, goes out into fierce wind, hands shaking on her purse but determined to beg a hundred dollars from her parents to go to Kansas City and take the required steps.

⁂

Going up the stairs in the dark office building, heavy heels clomping on the linoleum, Edith is frightened; she hopes her plan is reasonable, that the lawyer will see the need, the rightness of it. That he will accept the hundred dollars her parents have loaned her. She can ask for no more.

She has chosen this lawyer because of the bright blue sign, *F. Daily Law Firm,* so official and experienced-looking, and because the shop window next to his door showed placards advertising Ingrams Milkweed Cream, ExLax—"the laxative that tastes like chocolate"—and a stack of Ivory soap, all things she is familiar with and has used. A sense of comfort made opening the door onto the staircase easier.

The stairs are dark and smell like her father's barn, horse piss and straw; she finds it difficult to breathe. She controls her urge to run back outside into the spring day with its breezes and the energizing clatter of streetcars and the rush of men in their stiff suits and women, some in stylish hats. Only the thought of her girls makes her continue. And yes, Milton! Thin as a cornstalk, but at least he is in the hospital now with a doctor she trusts, a doctor recommended by their own Enterprise doctor. She repeats her daily mantra. *Please Lord, help him to get well. You know I love him. Doris and Mildred need a father. Amen.*

In the office, the lawyer's clerk stands in front of a bookcase with a glass window protecting each shelf. One of the windows is open and the smell of leather bindings is a relief after the stairway. "Excuse me, I wish to speak to Mr. Franklin Daily."

Dropping the window in front of the books, the young man turns and says, "I am he."

My goodness, he is young, hair slicked back with Brilliantine, face unlined, no sign of strain, untouched by war or terrible events. How can he understand her problem? His jacket looks like a schoolboy's; she needs a man to challenge the government. Before she can flee, the young man quickly pulls out a chair. "Please sit here, madam."

She understands he doesn't want to lose a client.

"How may I help you?"

His voice is older than his face and his polite gesture somewhat soothes her. Still, she doesn't sit. "It's about my husband." Mr. Daily's face twitches. Does he think Milton has run off? Or been injured in a factory? Perhaps he doesn't take such cases. "He was in the war," Edith continues quickly. "The war has ruined him and he is unable to work." Her voice wavers, she clenches her teeth. "The government has refused to pay his insurance. We—I mean myself and my two daughters—are quite destitute."

He gestures toward the chair again, bowing.

Edith walks to the chair, tiptoeing slightly to keep her heels silent on the wooden floor; when she sits, not touching the chair back, it squeaks under her weight. "You are a licensed lawyer? I must be certain; my case is of such importance."

"Madam, all cases are important. However . . ." He walks to the wall, takes down a framed certificate and holds it before her.

Yes, he graduated from the University of Missouri. Somewhat mollified, she slides back slightly on the seat. "You have been in court?"

"Why yes, Mrs . . .?"

"Fieth. What sort of case have you taken?" She feels she may need more support than this slight young man can supply, but as he walks to his desk, she sees he has a long stride. That and his voice reassure her.

"I cannot divulge my current caseload, of course, but I recently sued the city and won a large sum for a local river company on the occasion of fraudulent claims regarding conditions at their worksites."

Fraudulent claims sounds to Edith similar to what she has experienced. Besides, is she to go down those awful stairs and walk up and down the streets again, looking for another sign? No, no, she can't face it.

"You understand I need money to support my young daughters, Mildred and Doris." She leans forward and places the candy box she has been holding onto Mr. Daily's desk. "There is no insanity in my husband's family, and he is no coward, no matter what others may think. Shell shock, that's what it is. I don't understand why no one will admit that the Great War shattered him. Why people talk, saying unkind . . ." She twists slightly away and covers her mouth.

Mr. Daily says nothing.

"I've had to place my husband in hospital. His mind is broken. He cannot work and we are destitute." She leans forward and grips the edge of his desk. "I wish to sue the United States Government for the reinstatement of my husband's pension upon the circumstance of his ruination in the war."

JUNE 1937, MILTON

KANSAS CITY HOSPITAL, KANSAS

After his breakdown, Milton wakens in a Kansas City hospital where his first year passes like a troubled dream: hydrotherapy and rounds of electric shocks after weeks of screaming nightmares–kicking Herbert, blood smearing his hands, attacked by swooping evil birds whose beaks fire like guns. At weekly sessions with a doctor trained in the newfangled psychotherapy, he refuses to talk about the war, something the doctor at the Jefferson Barracks emphasized years ago. So the new doctor asks endlessly about his childhood, and Milton pulls up memories of his mother's pie, of running to the outhouse across frosty grass and the smell of plowed fields, of laughter when the hay wagon almost tipped over, and of cheering a little colt staggering to its feet. "Hold onto those thoughts," the doctor says.

He also reassures Milton the nightmares and the shaking are beyond his conscious control but that he can gain weight if he puts his mind to it. Milton tries, ashamed of his girlish wrist bones and the rack of ribs other men see in the shower, but food sticks in his throat and remembering rations, he's unable to swallow.

He rouses when Edith comes for a week in the summer to sit by his bed and take his hand, connecting him to the pillar of her bulk, her safety. When she mentions the lawyer who is fighting for his pension, he wants to thank her but he's embarrassed. His wife shouldn't have to worry. He wants to be the man. Days when his mind is clear, he shakes with wrath. The government sent him to war without a blink and now they don't care that his head is in disarray. The treatments are useless; a mind isn't like a farm machine. He needs his family. When Edith leaves, he cries into his pillow, then faces the dragging hours.

December approaches, and he realizes his girls have birthdays. He wants to go home to see them and have cake, but the doctor says he's not strong enough yet. Did the doctor mean his body or his mind? He sends them cards. He still can't eat.

The second year Edith comes to stay for a month and he's more alert—less medicine—and he thanks her right away. She says, "I'm your wife." Her words dip out happy memories and they embrace. "My, I need to fatten you up." She has brought boxes of cookies, his favorites: sugar scented with anise, chocolate rocks, date swirls. When he asks how the girls are keeping, she says she's sent them to Missouri to be with his family; he tries to remember how old they are but he can't, and it blocks his voice. Before she returns to her rented room at the end of the day, Edith gives him three cookies wrapped in a napkin. He saves one for breakfast and eats the others leaning over the side of the bed so as not to get crumbs in the sheets. He gains seven pounds but when she goes back to Enterprise, he quickly loses them.

In the third and final year of his hospitalization, Edith stays with him for two months. "Your daughters are running wild in Missouri with your folks," she says, and gives him the letters they've written and cookies, including oatmeal raisin and brownies. His gift for gab returns and he gains sixteen pounds. She jokes he won't blow away and rolls him out onto the patio in a wheelchair where he rediscovers the wonders of blue sky and grass. And the silence! Outside, his brain expands, floating in the warmth outside his skull. His toes unclench; he breathes in sweetness from the peonies. Inside, men yell in pain or horror, carts clank down the corridors, nurses run past on squeaky shoes, radios blare in the evenings. The noise pins him. He can't move or think.

His weight gain and the lessening of nightmares convince the doctor that Milton needs the constant support of his wife, and he's sent home. Edith picks him up in an old Chevy, saying, "A gift from Uncle Wallis, something extra on his car lot," and Milton knows his family has thanked her. "This will be more comfortable for you than the train," Edith says, but when they drive out of the parking lot, the world swirls past and he can't grab hold of it. Shaking rattles his torso and he asks her to stop, climbs in the back, and stretches out on the seat. Edith turns on the little radio. When news comes on, she pushes a button for another station. They are listening to Glenn Miller when Milton falls asleep and when he wakes, they are in front of the house where Edith lived when he first met her. She has said it belonged to them now, given by his in-laws, but still he's surprised.

The house smells of baking and dust rising through the heating grid in the floor. He asks where the girls are, and Edith says, "Doris and Mildred are going downtown to have a soda after school. I thought you might want a little quiet time to settle in."

At first, the house is as foreign as France. Scents of perfume, shoe polish, soap, then in the kitchen, familiar cinnamon slows his heartbeat. Edith shows him the green cookie jar. Says he can eat as many cookies as he wants. He takes a chocolate rock and steps out onto the screened back porch, shrugging sideways past the hulking washing machine, and opens the door. Flowers. The long backyard stretching down to the alley. He recognizes a bush like one his mother kept, billowing with blooms. Edith says she will put a chair for him in the yard if he wants. He nods and takes her hand.

His daughters arrive, full-grown and surprising; he can scarcely look at them, somehow expecting younger, shorter children. Their dresses scramble his eyes: Doris's skirt is striped in all directions and held up with striped suspenders, Mildred's dress is dotted with huge buttons. They offer hesitant kisses, then Edith says, "Go wash up. We're having your father's favorite, fried chicken. Aren't we glad he's home?" She leans lightly against him.

Doris says, "I'll set the table." Mildred says, "I'll help." As they escape the room, Mildred turns back to say, "I made pie." Milton grins, letting old ghosts rise and fade. He's almost reluctant to lose Herbert, his friend, but no; he wants them to stay gone.

DECEMBER 1940, EDITH

ENTERPRISE, KANSAS

To Edith's relief, Milton has returned to talking, not the jabber his family once described, but enough. He never mentions the war going on in Europe, but some of his ideas surprise her. He suggests they plant blackberries for pie and save pennies in a Mason jar. He also says Mildred will never make it through school, unlike Doris who's always with a book. It breaks her heart how little he knows. Doris is a dreamer, the books are for escape, not learning. Mildred is steady. But Milton missed so many years and can't really see his daughters. She yearns to find a way to help him get closer to them.

Doris is a sophomore at the local college; Mildred became a freshman in September. Edith has been determined they will have a way to support their coming lives; they will never be destitute. Although Milton's pension is barely enough to live on, Edith has scrimped and, with her parents' help, found money to send them. She doesn't want to dictate what they study, but she worries about Doris who's taking journalism. She really wants to write, but she claims no one in Kansas writes books, so she plans to work at *The Enterprise Journal* when she graduates. Edith is hoping she'll stay home, maybe marry a nice local boy—though none come to mind—but Doris is restless and Edith is prepared for her leaving. Mildred, serious, responsible, and modern, plans to study business with the hope of opening a store over in Abilene.

If Edith had her way, they'd both take the excellent teachers' course offered by Emporia College and get steady dependable jobs, but what's a mother to do if her children are adamant? At some point they must make their own decisions. Edith smiles remembering her own mother's resignation when she announced her engagement to Milton.

One Sunday, with the girls home for Christmas and the whole family together, she sits on the sofa to read the Abilene paper while her daughters are doing the dishes. The pictures of London bombed in what everyone is calling "The Blitz" show whole blocks burned to the ground, mothers digging through the rubble for their children, little orphaned boys and girls crying on street corners. Truthfully, the photos don't contain children, but she knows in her heart that's the way war is. She puts down the paper, shuts her eyes, and prays. When she opens them, she smiles at Milton reading the funnies and overhears an argument in the kitchen.

"You promised," Mildred says. "Too late to change your mind." In answer, a pot crashes onto the counter. "I don't care if you're tired." Mildred again. "You have to come." This time it's a clatter of silverware, then Mildred wails, "You promised."

"I want to put on slippers and lollygag tonight," Doris says loudly. "I'm in the middle of a good book." A cupboard door slams. "Can I go in slippers?"

"No, and comb your hair. You look like a hooligan."

An hour later two young men arrive, thumping across the front porch. Doris jumps up from her book. "Shoes. I need shoes." Mildred smooths her wool skirt and straightens her pearls before she opens the door. "Hello, Dean. Philip."

Both men carry hats dusted with snow and wear tan sweaters with ties, but Edith sees it will be easy to keep them apart. Mildred's date is tall, with curly brown hair. Philip, for Doris, is almost as tall, but his hair is darker and his ears stick out. During his introduction—"Philip Byram studies chemistry. Potions, not prescriptions. A straight-A genius"—he stands restlessly, unabashed, looking as if he were going to tell a joke. As soon as Mildred stops speaking, he reaches out eagerly to shake Milton's hand. "Sir," he says.

Edith suppresses the urge to pat his shoulder and tell him to calm down, he wasn't asking for her hand in marriage.

Milton says, "Where are you taking our daughters?"

"Over to Salina for a movie. Afterwards supper. If you don't mind."

Milton looks at Edith. She nods. "Well, that's all right then."

Philip is still shifting from foot to foot and Edith realizes he's wondering where his date is. "Doris," she calls, "they're waiting for you."

"Just a minute." Edith can tell by the tone that Doris is not in a cooperative mood. An open book on the chair signals she's been ripped from a story she wants to finish.

"We'll miss the beginning of the movie." Mildred heads toward the bedroom and bumps into Doris coming out, shoes on, hat jammed on her head; her red plaid jacket clashes with her orange skirt. "Nice to meet you, Dean. Philip." She heads out the door, grabbing Milton's discarded funny papers from the arm of the couch. "Hope you don't mind if I bring these along."

Philip is after her like a shot. "You'll have to share. I like *Krazy Kat*."

Edith chuckles, almost calls out, "Good luck." Doris tends to the romantic: *Prince Valiant*, *Mary Worth*, and *Brenda Starr*. She dreams of being a reporter like Brenda, traveling the world; she'll never stand for a plain Kansas boy, straight A's or not.

After the car drives off, Edith says, "How about another piece of pie?" Milton is too slim for her taste; it's all the walking, because he eats plenty.

"Sure, if you'll join me."

She doesn't want more pie; the mirror shows her to be a stout woman with graying hair, and although she can do nothing about the gray, she could lessen the stout. But Milton will say no if she doesn't join him. She decides to have hers without cream. They move to the kitchen and sit at the little table by the window, eating and chatting about the young men.

Edith waits up for her daughters. It's late when they arrive but she asks about the movie. Doris declares great; Mildred, boring. "Well, which?" Like children, they talk over each other, but in whispers because their father's in bed.

"I couldn't understand a word; they talked so fast."

"It was about a reporter."

"And a divorce. They got back together."

"It was so funny. Cary Grant told her, 'You've got the brain of a pancake.'"

"If they were going to get back together, why divorce in the first place?"

"She'd have been unhappy with that other guy, a complete wimp, and Cary Grant is so handsome."

"Pushy and loud. He played the ex-husband, Mother."

Edith is laughing, "My goodness. What was the movie called?"

"*His Girl Friday*," the girls say in unison.

Mildred kisses her mother's cheek and goes to bed. Doris sits on the footstool by the chair where she left her book, stretching her legs into the room. "Philip thought the movie was funny." She giggles. "'You've got the brain of a pancake.'"

"I'm glad you had a good time." Edith notices how Doris is lolling on the footstool with the look of a rainbow on her face and realizes, my goodness, this had been more than a good time. "What else did you do?"

"We had a snowball fight. You know how I can never hit anyone? I got Philip on the shoulder and on the back." Edith can see how important this is to Doris. "Well, good for you, dear. How was his aim?"

"He missed and missed and missed." Doris is smiling; she looks wide-awake, alert.

"Well, your father's waiting for me. I'm off to bed. Don't forget to turn out the light." As Edith leaves the room, Doris rises, twirls, giggles again, and flops full length on the couch with her wet shoes still on. Edith doesn't bother to comment.

SEPTEMBER 1941, MILTON

ENTERPRISE, KANSAS

Winter and spring pass, the girls come home again for the summer, then it's fall and they return to college and their chatter and plans vanish. With them gone, Milton develops a routine to calm the inner shudders that rise when he's in the house with nothing to do. He makes the bed then breakfasts with Edith, talking over coffee. When his leg begins to jiggle uncontrollably, he says, "I believe I'll go out for a short walk," puts his coffee cup in the sink, dons his hat, and takes a quarter from the little dish on the sideboard. He'd been home for a year when Edith said, "You shouldn't have to ask me for money. It's your pension we live on. I'll just put change here and you can take what you need." He's proud she knows he can manage.

Some mornings Edith asks him to pick up a pound of ground beef and hands him a dollar, but today she just kisses his cheek. Thank goodness. Last week the butcher thwacked down his knife as Milton entered, and only squeezing his eyes shut and fisting his hands against his chest maintained his normality.

Pushing down the war, the blood and bombs, exhausts him but he must. He doesn't want to go back to the hospital.

As usual he goes out the back door, across the yard past the derelict garage where wasps buzz and dive bomb. He knows he should knock them down but has been unable to. He turns down the alley toward town. He likes it, the alley, because it gives him time to ready for neighborly encounters on 2nd Street. He practices, clearing his throat and nodding—"Nice to meetcha"—at a crossing cat.

Five blocks to Main on a perfect day, sidewalks empty, sky pouring serene blue. On Main, he'd usually go north out of town to the Smoky Hill River and the old iron bridge—what a work of engineering—and stand over the silent water, surveying the fields, breathing in the scent of dirt as wind rustled the crops. But harvesting has started. Threshing machines pulverize the earth like ghastly tanks, lumbering, cacophonous, swiveling their guns, impelling him to run, to scream. No, he can't risk it.

Instead, he goes south to the post office, where Mrs. Ersham, the post mistress, is sorting mail into the orderly rows of little boxes fronted by glass doors secured with combination locks. He says, "Good morning, it's a beaut out there," and she responds, "And so it is, Mr, Fieth." She comes out from behind the boxes. "Sunshine's good for a body. Say, did I hear your eldest is seeing a K-State man?" Milton opens his box, nodding slightly, unwilling to say that Doris appears completely enamored with the boy. "Young fellas moving mighty fast nowadays. Girls need to be on guard, though Doris has a good head on her shoulders." Letters in his pocket, he tips his hat and leaves for the drug store to sit at the counter where he has another cup of coffee and a slice of the Dutch apple pie displayed on the counter. Walt, who runs the place, knows Milton's history and talks only of farms and crop yields and the farm board meetings.

Restored, he loops home past the park, empty now that the children are back in school. He misses the happy voices, the giggles and swinging and taking turns on the slide that has a hump in the middle, over which the brave ones go so fast their little bottoms lift in the air and all the children holler. At first, the holler sounded to him like "over the top" and he'd flee into the street, but now he recognizes when it's coming and is prepared and can laugh at the hijinks. One particular scamp always pulls off the trick; Milton loves him. Also, the little girl who can do the same trick, her long braids flying out like lassoes.

Today he sits on the merry-go-round and stares up through the trees thinking of the war grinding across Europe, far away, yes, but he feels it in his gut—countries destroyed, men spit out like sausage, and although he pushes and pushes the thought down, he's joined by Herbert, his smell of tobacco, his cough, his accusation: *You kicked me when I was dying in the trench.* Milton grips the rail, shuddering. "I'm sorry, you know, but I couldn't . . ." He starts to rise but a breath on his neck cracks open a memory of his best friend sliding down his chest, the blood and fear. "I should have stayed . . ." His voice shakes. A distant train whistle pierces him. "But it was over the top or desertion." He's afraid to turn his head and see his friend's face, but then recess arrives over at the grade school and children run out shouting, laughing, he can hear their joy, and Herbert eases away.

Milton sits until behind his eyelids is only a faint wash of sun and he can go home to ask Edith like a concerned father if she thinks this thing with Philip and Doris is going too fast.

JANUARY 1942, EDITH

ENTERPRISE, KANSAS

When wind rattles the stained glass, the entire congregation shivers. Edith tugs her old wool coat around her knees, noticing the bits of pulled fabric like little flags. She's had this coat for six years, bought after she'd won the suit against the government and the veteran's checks began arriving on a regular basis. In a few weeks, she'll put it into the church's missionary box because back at the house is a nice blue tweed, a Christmas gift from Doris and Philip, cut out and ready to be sewn into a warmer version of the one she now wears. For the new coat, Mildred gave her Lucite buttons, very much in fashion, somewhat showy for Edith's taste, but she'll use them.

The congregation stands for the scripture and the pastor reads from the book of Joel in the Old Testament: "*Prepare war, wake up the mighty men, let all the men of war draw near; let them come up. Beat your plowshares into swords, and your pruning hooks into spears.*"

War again. The Japanese flying from their tiny island all the way to Hawaii. She thinks of the boys lying under the water in their ships and shudders. She's never seen a Japanese person; why would they attack? More destruction. More dying. She understands the need to defend the country but what about the Kansas men and yes, Philip, who has graduated and intends to enlist after the wedding, all of them marching off to killing? And why did Milton fight if the suffering was to be repeated so soon? The scant history she remembers from school taught her that war is inevitable—the Romans, the Crusades, the Thirty Years War in England or was it France? But what can God be thinking; the world needs time to rest and recover between spasms. She quickly asks forgiveness. He has a plan for the world, for Philip, Doris, Mildred. And Milton.

She distracts herself with the stained glass, entwined flowers around the edges of the window and the lamb with a red-robed Jesus, calm and in peace. She's glad the church hasn't changed since she was a girl, a surety in the chaos of living.

Hortense sits a few pews down, collar turned up. Fur. Not rabbit, but real otter or maybe even mink. Clarence is doing well; the mercantile had been packed before Christmas, geegaws and tinsel piled alongside the socks and wooden spoons, all of it selling as if the world was coming to an end (which it might be) and there'd never be another chance to gift a son with a tie (which also might be true). On busy days, Hortense helped at the counter, wrapping muffin tins and packets of embroidery thread in plain paper, her rings glittering. Edith's glad for her friend, although there are more important things than fur or rings. Children, for instance. Hortense is childless, a matter of great distress to her and her family, but when the doctor said there was no hope, Clarence added a sleeping porch to their house and took his wife for a trip to Florida. Hortense has never mentioned it since, although she always remembers Doris and Mildred on their birthdays and has volunteered to provide a cake for the wedding. She also ordered the special satin and seed pearls Edith will use to sew Doris's dress.

The wind changes, bringing a slight hiss of snow pellets on the glass; Edith hears it clearly over the pastor's words, "We must gird ourselves against the coming storm; we must prepare to help our friends who are suffering." She can't save the world. Only her own family. She glances down the pew to her daughters and soon-to-be son-in-law.

Behind her, someone sneezes violently. Had Milton been here, he'd have been out the door or under the pew. He's mostly well, able to talk and smile and walk—he'll give Doris away at the wedding—but he cannot abide crowds or loud noises. She assumes he never will, but she thanks the Lord for letting him have this short time with his girls.

After the final "Go in peace," the pastor stands inside the church door, shaking hands with his congregants. Edith is just leaving when Hortense calls, "Hidee-ho." The young people escape, but Edith waits as her friend comes gingerly down the snow-slushed steps. "I was looking to see if you had completed your new coat. Such up-to-date fabric and those buttons. The very latest in style. Your daughters have such outstanding taste.

I was telling Clarence that you have been well rewarded after all that striving to bring Milton home and win his monthly pittance. And Philip! Doris has made a brilliant match; top of his class and so handsome."

Edith knows Hortense means well, but heavens, how she talks. "How is Clarence?"

"Flourishing but for a slight case of chilblains that forced him away from church this morning. He promised to remove the roast when it was perfection."

Clarence will never come to church—week after week there are excuses made and accepted—but to each his own. A quote from Shakespeare? She remembers reading it in high school with amazement, the idea that a person could choose. She felt herself surrounded by farmers, farmers, and more farmers with their wives and the same conversation and the same worries: babies, crops, broken machines, weather. None of them seeming to be their *own*. She had vowed to be different then, never thinking how difficult *different* could be, or how that difference might not be wholly of her own choosing.

"Can I offer you transport?" Hortense seldom walks.

"Thank you, but no. The air is so fresh."

"Ravishingly so. Mind you don't slip. The snow is dangerous, even in boots."

Edith goes the long way through the park, using the time to plan the wedding dress. She'll fill the neckline with tulle, edge it with seed pearls, and stitch a row of buttons down the back so the dress looks lovely when Doris faces the altar.

At home, she finds Philip sprawled in the living room on the couch studying. In the small dining room where they only eat on Sundays, Mildred is folding napkins for each place; in the kitchen, Doris stands by the stove, stirring gravy and making flirty faces at her fiancé.

Edith hangs up her coat, lays her scarf out to dry, checks for Milton. He's not in the house. A moment of panic as of old. She hopes he's out walking; he gets restless, pent up, and she worries even though he's steadier now. She wants him in charge of some part of his life. He helps with the dishes and makes the bed, but he needs something for his pride. She has been casting around for a suitable job, not in an office or that requires driving, and thinks she has found a possibility.

In the kitchen, she nudges Doris away from the gravy which is beginning to lump and takes over stirring. With a swoosh of fresh air, Milton comes in the back door, his hair iced up into a wild pompadour, his smile real, his feet stamping on the linoleum. "Cold enough to freeze your teeth, Edith?" he laughs. "Is that chicken I smell? Any chance of pie?"

"Apple," says Mildred. "I made apple."

"There's real cream from Grandma Borgman," says Doris.

"A feast." Milton hangs his coat on the hook by the door. "C'mon young man," he calls to Philip. "Let's eat. The sooner we start, the sooner we get to our treats."

After dessert—the pie a great success—the young people go out to meet friends and Edith refills the coffee cups. "Milton, I've been thinking."

He stiffens. "Sounds like trouble." He draws circles on the plate with his fork, metal tines squeaking. She pushes on. "In the newspaper, I see companies looking for people to sell their products. Magazine subscriptions or such like. Malinda told me that Warrenton is so overrun with door-to-door salesmen, you can scarcely sit down to supper but some fellow's knocking, trying to get you to buy a brush or a tonic; however, I've never seen one here in Enterprise. Seems like it would be something you'd enjoy."

"Are you needing me out of the house?" Milton's voice is soft with an edge of wheeze. "I can be more of a help if you'd let me."

"You help plenty, but you like to walk. And you talk so kindly to people. I think you could be a big success." She knows she must be careful, to build up his positive feelings, not make him feel like he's unwanted. Years ago, the doctor said, "Let him talk freely, but be careful what you say to him." She has tried to follow that advice, speaking adult to adult, unlike some of the shop owners in town who use a forced brightness that says, *You're crazy but I'm a good person and can ignore it.*

The scraping continues. She lays down her own fork, willing him to follow suit, and waits.

"Would I have to carry a load of magazines?" Not quite a whisper, but close.

"I can write and find out if you're interested." He won't want to pack a load of samples. Anything reminiscent of war is shunned: canteens, drab green shirts, meat in tins, heavy loads. His mental state has diminished his life, forcing him away from travel and groups of people, but the only other choice is to have him in the hospital where he'd be even more confined. Better that he be home where they can cuddle in the night and she can stroke his arm when he begins to flail with bad dreams because the dreams haven't entirely gone away. He says they're better now, sometimes he can watch them like a movie as if they mean nothing. She's glad he suffers less.

She reaches out to touch his hand. "No need to decide now. Think about it for a while."

MAY 1943, MILTON

ENTERPRISE, KANSAS

Milton cuts short his walk and goes straight to town. Months ago his new son-in-law left for officer training while Doris, then pregnant, chose to stay home with Edith and her own doctor, but now the baby's old enough to travel and today they leave for California where Philip's stationed. Milton understands the family needs to be together, but he's worried about the long train ride and unkind people when Nan cries. He'd forgotten how much babies cry. His other worry: what if Nan grows up and doesn't remember him? He can't bear trains or planes, California is too far to ask Edith to drive, and gas is rationed. Something to remember him by, that's what he needs.

In the mercantile, Clarence steps out from behind the display case to shake Milton's hand. "What can I do for you, Miltie?"

He'd been counting on Hortense, forgetting she'd be at the farewell party. What does Clarence know about baby girls? With no other choice, Milton forges ahead. "I want to buy a present for Nan." In his pocket, the money he has earned selling subscriptions. "Something special."

Clarence, evidently trained by Hortense, shows him a pink checked blanket, a tiny bonnet, a crocheted dress, a stuffed rabbit with real fur, and a hard rattle. Ha! The man knows nothing; the baby might hit herself with the rattle, the way her arms wave about. Milton settles on the rabbit—soft like her. He has never actually held Nan, afraid his past will rise up and he'll drop her, but he has touched her cheek. How can such delicacy exist? "Wrap it in something pretty." Clarence offers yellow tissue or blue-flowered paper. He chooses yellow for cheer.

At the post office he picks up mail, and Mrs. Ershom gives him a bouquet of early peonies from her garden: "For the party." He walks home with a sense of finality, of last hugs and goodbyes, regretting all the things he could have and should have done and in the midst of this loss, the past throws him into the trench and he hears, "This is it, Miltie. The real thing." He almost drops the flowers, but no, he brings them to his face and their scent chokes Herbert's voice.

The bouquet allows him to edge into the group gathered within his house: Hortense, Walt from the drugstore, Mildred home from university where she's a senior in the nursing course, even his sister Malinda come from Missouri and now speaking to Edith. Talk is soft because the baby's sleeping in a bassinette in the middle of the front room. Doris leaves her friends and comes to hug him, then pulls a young woman over. "Daddy, this is my best friend from high school." He's never seen the girl before and is stunned; he'd missed so much, spending years in the hospital. Now he stammers out, "Nice to meetcha." And she smiles. As they talk, he hears with alarm she studies business, surely not appropriate for a young woman—Mildred sensibly gave up that idea—but he stays silent. Others come to greet him; his sister pulls him aside, whispering Missouri news: a new car, two nieces married, a broken finger.

When the baby stirs, the crowd converges on the bassinette, cooing and smiling. Doris lifts Nan and sits on the sofa. Edith takes Milton's arm. "Come sit. They are going to take a family picture." Doris's friend who has the camera says, "Smile. Hold the baby up. Everyone look at her." Milton looks and the baby looks back with round dark eyes, and he can't help reaching out and Doris settles Nan on his lap before he has time to withdraw.

His granddaughter. He tries to memorize her face, the dip below her nose leading to little bow lips. He touches his own scar, glad she's perfect. When she yawns, he chuckles, wants to take a nibble of her cheek. Doris will bring her to visit Edith and when she's old enough, he'll take her to the playground and teach her to fly on the slide. Or to the drugstore, her legs dangling from the stool, drinking a Dr. Pepper. He'll buy her roller skates and shiny shoes and movie tickets. He touches the baby's cheek with his finger and she grins at him; he looks up with delight to see if anyone noticed, and across the room stands Herbert, freckled and sunburned as he was before the war. Milton holds out the baby. "See my granddaughter. I'm sorry."

Doris takes the child from him. "Time for a diaper change?"

Missing the weight on his lap, Milton vows to always be there for Nan, no matter what. Like Edith has been for him.

AUGUST 10, 1945, EDITH & MILTON

ENTERPRISE, KANSAS

A fan labors in the front room where Edith sits with Hortense, drinking iced tea. Their discomfort is not only the August heat and the noise; they are talking about Hiroshima and Nagasaki, the latter obliterated two days ago.

"An atomic bomb," exclaims Hortense. "What can that even mean? I remember atoms from science class. They ran in rings around a little center and I imagined a tiny carousel with organ music. Now we find they're deadly. My heart bleeds for those buried in their collapsed houses, but then they were the architects of their own destruction. Look at how they refused to give up."

Edith merely nods. She wishes that Milton hadn't gone out this morning. That Hortense would be kinder.

"They are now well and truly beaten, thank goodness, but those photos! I actually tremble when picking up a newspaper. The mushroom cloud and cities like garbage dumps."

Edith sighs. "I keep thinking about the young men who dropped the bombs. How they must feel, causing such death."

Hortense pats her face with a pristine hankie. "I am somewhat surprised our president has proven so vengeful. One bomb would surely have sufficed." She tucks the hankie in her belt. "How's Milton taking it?"

"He seemed calm when he left for his morning walk. You know how he loves the outdoors." Edith glances at the clock on the sideboard. 10:47. She'll have time to make egg salad before lunch. "I have some good news. Doris called Sunday."

"Oh, how delightful! So intelligent to call on the weekend when it's cheaper." Hortense sips her tea. "What did she report?"

"They have settled in Pasadena, not Los Angeles. Philip bought a car, an old '39 Chevy. Evidently you must have a car in California. Doris says it doesn't have a heater, but it's so warm there, they won't miss it." Far away, she hopes her granddaughter is toddling in the summer dress she sewed and sent.

"I long to visit California, but the train, my dear, is so crowded."

Milton knows Edith is protecting him— she turns off the news and hides the papers—but he senses the violent world in her tightened lips, her crossed arms. He needs the fields, the gentle swoosh of wheat waving at the sky. Body jerking, he marches quick-step to the iron bridge and leans on the railing, face lifted to the amber fields, trying to breathe away the knots in his chest.

Beneath his feet the water flows smoothly, not a single rill. Overhead, bird song. He arches back, the sky pours blue, he closes his eyes to peace, then hangs over the rail, arms reaching toward the water. He decides to walk out into the rustling wheat.

He has crossed the bridge when a car roars up from behind, horn blasting. Startled, he jumps aside. The driver guns the engine and zooms away, waving. Milton freezes, almost screams as the driver's hand releases a gigantic bird that swoops low over his head like a small plane. He falls to his knees, chest thudding, but the bird evanesces. He stares across the field to the swaying wheat, struggling to summon the strength of the last three years–selling magazines, ducking into the drugstore for coffee, coming home to Edith. After a moment, he manages to push down memories of mud, tanks, bombs, rain, blood. His heart continues to clench and twist under his ribs, but he begins to breathe better.

He turns toward town. He'll visit the drugstore and buy something for Edith. Lilac talc or maybe a little blue bottle of Evening in Paris. A thank you, a reassurance that he's fine.

)K

Although Hortense's glass is empty, Edith hesitates to offer more. She needs to fix lunch. Years ago the doctor said consistency would ease her husband's condition so they always eat directly at noon. She smiles slightly; she knows Milton's habits. Right now he's drinking coffee at the drugstore and if Hortense leaves soon, she can go down, stock up on the hard candies he loves, and walk home with him like a normal couple. She imagines his hand, warm and soft, and ignores the slight clot of worry in her throat—it's only the news, not Milton; she prays briefly for the dead on that faraway island.

"And how is that darling Nan? And Philip?"

Edith pours more tea. "Doris writes that Nan is walking and has started to chatter complete nonsense. Philip has been hired at the Jet Propulsion Laboratory. I don't understand his job, but the company is newly formed and evidently perfect for his learning. You remember he studied chemistry."

"Absolutely excelled, didn't he? I always found him too handsome to waste his life as a tiresome scientist, although his ears do stick out a titch. Doris must love him to move so far from home with your grandbaby."

"Of course she does. They've found a bungalow with a backyard close to his work and bought a sandbox for Nan." Edith notices with a jolt that the clock hands haven't moved. "She's promised to send pictures after the film's developed . . . I'm sorry Hortense, but what is the time? I seem to have forgotten to wind the clock."

"Oh my heavens, it's 11:35. I will be late for my women's auxiliary meeting, although I suppose there won't be a need for socks now the war is ending."

⁂

Milton joins the Friday shoppers crowding Main Street, men in hats, women wearing cheerful dresses and carrying bundles. He smells a cigar, hears a greeting. Here is real life. The noise, the bustle. He is heading for the drugstore, a man about his business, when two boys race past on bikes, hollering, veering wildly in and out of the crowd. A man shouts. A woman drops a package. Milton's heart clamors and he almost flees, but as the crowd settles, he pounds his chest into quiet. Sweating, he rubs at the pain sprinkling his neck. He needs to get home, Edith will worry. He'll skip the drugstore.

At the corner a little girl is selling raspberries and he stops. Edith loves raspberries for the color she says, even though the seeds stick in her teeth. The girl's hands are scratched from the picking and he imagines, no feels, the sharp thorns down his own arms. He shrugs against the pain and leans heavily on the table to buy a newspaper cone filled with fruit. The girl's brown eyes make him think of Nan way out in California and suddenly he wants to cry.

)X(

Hortense is leaving in a hurry and Edith is pleased. She can walk with Milton from town, but then her friend pauses on the porch. "I quite forgot. Have you time to copy out your pickled peach recipe? I have a bounteous crop."

Edith wills Milton to remain at the drugstore and goes into the kitchen. When she returns, recipe in hand, she asks again for the time, stands until Hortense drives away, then winds the clock. 11:50. No time now; he's certainly on his way home. As she gathers the tea glasses and runs dishwater, she pictures him downtown, strolling, enjoying the fine weather, lifting his hat to neighbors.

Milton gasps a thank you to the little girl, takes the cone of raspberries, heavier than he expected, and turns toward Edith and lunch. The road stretches long, wavering in the heat. He pushes himself, soldiering through his exhaustion. He is passing the playground when Herbert joins him; Milton waits for accusations, but his friend is silent, smiling and friendly.

"These are for my missus." Milton holds out the raspberries. "She'd love to meet you." Breathless, he slows. "A fine woman. My luck to . . . have found her." His heart coils under his ribs, a tight clock spring. Socks and Oberly have come up behind, joshing, canteens clanking. He hasn't seen his friends for so long and he invites them all home for cookies. "Edith bakes. Sugar. Chocolate." His inner spring twists and he clenches. "She takes care . . ." He limps down the alley, into the backyard. The house wavers. Dims. He longs to see her. To give her his gift, his love.

Edith checks the clock. 12:20. Milton's early years crash into her memory, the fleeing, the long stare. He should be here. She drops her dishtowel, rushes to the back door, and there he is, staggering across the yard, scattering red berries like drops of blood on the grass. She rushes onto the stoop, down the steps.

※

Milton's heart spring explodes when Herbert claps him on the back. "This is it, Miltie, the real thing." Chest shattered, he falters, lurches forward, reaching for Edith. She flies into the yard, catches him, eases him to the earth, cradling his head. "Oh my dearest love." She brushes his cheek with hers. His body is light in her arms, floating away. "Oh my dear, stay, stay with me." His eyes flicker to hers, his face opens with joy, then he's gone.

AUGUST 1950, DORIS

PASADENA, CALIFORNIA, TO ENTERPRISE, KANSAS

Doris sits on the back porch stoop watching Nan leap around the yard, practicing for ballet class. When the phone rings, she dusts off her hands and goes into the kitchen, expecting to hear that the library book she put on hold is available. But it's Hortense, sobbing. "Edith was outside hanging laundry. The sun, so dreadfully hot, simply burning and I looked out." A gust of sobs. "She was actually crumpled on the ground." When Doris understands her mother has died, her world stills. She suffers through a description of the scattered clothespins and the serenity on her mother's face, then says, "I'll call Mildred. Please call the pastor." She hangs up, tries to breathe, but tears pool. Another heart attack. Five years since her father's. Nan will never know that her grandmother loved the smell of sheets dried in the sun. Never have another special cookie, never . . . Nan bursts in. "I'm hungry, Mommy." Doris gathers herself, makes lunch, then sets Nan up cutting out paper dolls. All through the afternoon as she makes the many calls, an image of her mother squinting in the sunshine stays with her.

⋇

At the funeral, Doris sits with her family in the familiar church, holding Mildred's hand and shushing Nan, who comments loudly about Jesus's red dress.

A day of cake and condolences—Hortense kind and oddly silent—then the house must be cleared out for sale. Philip takes Nan to the playground or sits with her on the front porch reading stories while Doris and Mildred work, donating, discarding, choosing what to keep. Mildred takes the little record player, a lace tablecloth, and a stack of towels for her apartment but, because of a new job over in the Topeka hospital, must leave before they've finished; Doris continues alone.

On the last day, Doris accepts Hortense's offer to look after Nan and goes to the house with Philip, who wants to check the closets one last time. They can wait together for the antique dealer to pick up the sprawling Victorian sideboard.

On the sidewalk, Doris clutches her Enterprise life. Or rather, it clutches her. Chasing fireflies while her mother sat on the porch swing—now sold. Scaring Mildred at night in the front bedroom by claiming the passing cars were growling tigers.

"Did you know Mother was born in this room?" Her voice echoes slightly.

"You've said." Philip opens the closet door. "Your grandmother, too, if I remember rightly."

"Think about the mess. Blood. Pots of boiling water, then baby Edith appears and squalls for the first time. I wonder if Granddad paced the living room."

"Hard to imagine your mother as a baby." He takes a tissue from his pocket and wipes the closet shelf. "Spotless."

Doris leans in the door frame, tantalizingly close to her mother's life, the long years of daily toil, cooking and baking unending cookies and pies. Dusting, scouring the old sink, beating the rugs with a grunt at each whack as the motes whirled away. Edith could light a fire in a stove and kill a chicken from the coop. She managed the ungainly washing machine with its hand-wringer on the back porch and hung the clothes on a line. Again the image of her standing in the sun, sheet damp against her cheek.

And now the house is blank. The heavy black telephone on the desk, gone. The green water pitcher in the fridge, the frayed bedspread, the pile of heavy-heeled shoes, also black, all gone. Their life here now preserved only in stories and tiny black-and-white photos. Her mother the calm center, firm as her girdle, loving as homemade cookies. Her father the valiant soldier carrying the war inside. With a familiar pang, Doris wishes she'd known him better. Paid more attention when he finally came home.

"Was selling the right thing?" She leans against Philip.

"The only thing, honey. We can't fly out from L.A. once a year, spend a few days, then leave it to rot. It's old; it needs a lot of upkeep."

Her gut objects; her head rules. "Keep reminding me." They move through the bathroom with its stained tub and into her parents' bedroom. Where pictures have been removed, squares of unfaded wallpaper are like windows looking out to rosy bowers.

"Do you remember her lotion? A homemade witch hazel concoction she kept in a blue glass bottle without a stopper. She plugged it with a cotton ball. I hated to throw it away."

"I remember the ugly old tray with the braided edge."

"Nice try." She laughs. "It's coming home with us."

In the kitchen, the tray waits with the cookie jar, an embroidered silk hanky, and a doll with eyes that open and close.

"How are you going to carry all that on the train?"

"I was expecting some help." A tremor of loss catches in her throat; she swallows, picks up the doll. "I need to keep some things." She'll make a shelf in Pasadena to hold her longing for her mother. For Kansas, its vast unassuming and restful fields. California is bright and colorful with bold sun and surprising ferocious plants.

"Leave the tray. The other stuff will fit under the seat."

She hums deep in her throat, turns her back, and walks into the living room. "I'm keeping it all because I'm giving up this beauty." She touches the sideboard. "Mother kept chocolate in here when we had money. Other little surprises—a fold of orange tissue, quarters to go to the movies, once a slinky."

"Hmmm." He's opening drawers, sweeping his hand inside.

"I know. You've heard it before."

He rattles the middle drawer. "This is stuck. I thought you'd cleared everything out."

"I meant to mention it. It's probably empty." The past days of sorting, throwing away, driving loads to Abilene's thrift store, donating their mother's Bible to the Methodist church all press down on her. Suddenly overwhelmed, she sits on the floor, cradling the doll.

Philip pulls out a pocketknife to poke at the lock. His preparedness amazes her. She has married a boy scout. She's forgetful. She'd meant to pack the silken blouse, a Christmas gift, to wear at the funeral in honor of her mother who'd somehow held things together, but she'd left it in California. To quell tears, she snaps at Philip. "Don't mar the finish."

He glances at her with a moue and jimmies it open. "Aha." He hands her a dented tin candy box. "A treasure unearthed, madam."

She pries off the lid and spreads out the contents. A torn newspaper article about a ship delivering American soldiers to France. A discharge certificate from Jefferson Barracks Hospital. Her grandmother's handwriting and everywhere the name "Milton Fieth."

Philip picks up a sheet. "The Veterans Bureau sent money for travel to Iowa. For vocational training."

"We lived there when I was in second grade. Daddy was to raise chickens." She smooths the papers with shaking hands. "This is my family."

Two small brown photos slip free. Philip lifts a picture of two men in front of a brick building with tall windows and a small porch. Carved into the building: *Photographic Department, Bellevue*. "Is that your father?"

Doris is crying, the second photo pressed against her chest.

"Honey, what is it?" He takes it gently away.

"Me with Mildred on our birthday." She and her sister in bowl haircuts, holding cupcakes with candles. "Sitting on the porch steps at Bellevue."

"Oh, honey. Your father is so beaten."

"He didn't say a word all day. Mother tried to be cheerful, but we knew."

Philip pulls her close. "Your mother was a force of nature."

A workman knocks, calling through the screen. "Pickup for furniture."

They gather up the documents and the doll and watch as men wrestle the sideboard out the door, into the red truck, nestle it in padding, and drive away.

"That's it." Her body presses against his. "Let's get out of here." She can't stand another minute of the emptiness. They hurry to the rented car, pick up Nan, thank Hortense, and are on the train before she remembers the tray, the hankie, and the cookie jar left on the kitchen counter.

Outside the window, a windmill slides past. A dog barks at a farmhouse door. The train moves on and the house and dog disappear. She holds the candy box, Nan hums to the doll, Philip is coming down the aisle with a bottle of soda. She has both of them, her family. She vows to fill their lives with cookies and sewing and small celebrations and kindness, all the things she learned from her mother.

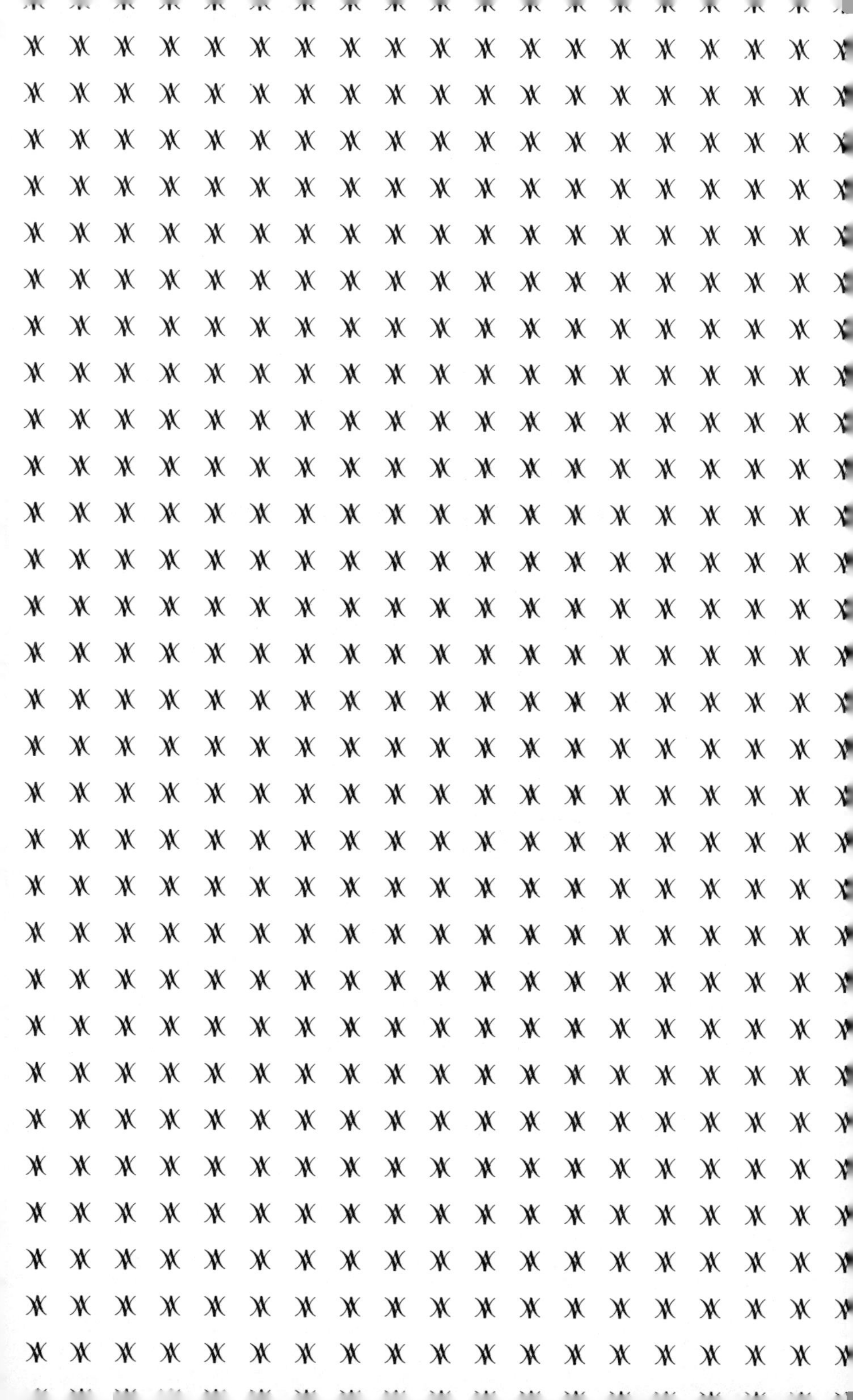

ACKNOWLEDGMENTS

When They Came Home is based on the lives of my grandparents. Long after I'd left college, my mother gave me a box of documents and photos, suggesting that as a writer, I might be interested in the contents. Weeks of sorting, of creating a timeline, revealed my grandmother's struggles when my grandfather returned from WWI with what was then called shell shock. We grandchildren had not been told of his breakdowns lest we become afraid of him, but we all sensed the strength and love of our grandmother.

Many of the objects and pictures referenced in the story are in my possession including the braided tray, the picture of the birthday party, Doris's wedding gown, the French silk hankie, and letters from the government and the lawyer. You can view them on my website terrilewis1.com under Artifacts.

I want to thank my editors, Joseph Bates and Sydney Bell; their sensitive reading and excellent suggestions made all the difference in this novel. Also Amina Gautier, judge of the 2025 Miami University Press Novella Prize, who thrillingly pulled my story from a pile of submissions. Jeff Clark, for his elegant cover. And finally to the many women writers whose critiques and belief in my writing have kept me afloat over the years, to my mother and aunt who shared personal stories of growing up with Milton and Edith, and most of all, my grandparents, whom I dearly loved. Now that I know their story, that love is tinged with awe at their courage and dignity. Their lives deserve to be celebrated.

After a career as a ballet dancer, Terri Lewis focused on writing. She is the author of *Behold the Bird in Flight: A Novel of an Abducted Queen*, a story inspired by the second wife of King John of Magna Carta fame. Her third novel will be published in March of '27. She lives in Denver with her husband and two entertaining dogs.